NOBLE SURRENDER

TÉ RUSS

Chapter One

"Noble! You made bail."

Ian Noble sat up on the stiff cot in the jail cell he'd been thrown in, letting his feet hit the disgusting, wet concrete floor.

His gaze stayed low as the sound of the lock unhinging, followed by the slow creaking of the bars automatically sliding open, filled the air.

The sound of shoes echoing against the walls drew closer to Ian. When the sound stopped, Ian's eyes locked onto the shoes; very expensive shoes.

A curse slipped from Ian's lips as his eyes went up from the two-toned, wing tipped, leather brogues, past the tailored designer suit, up to the face that looked identical to his.

Except his brother's countenance was a lot more pissed. No one else could tell by looking at Isaiah Noble. On the outside, he was simply calm and collected. But Ian could feel his brother's wrath threatening to boil over.

Ian placed his hands on his knees and pushed up onto his feet. Isaiah turned on his heels and led the way out of the jail cell.

A few seconds later, the sound of the bars to the cell he'd occupied for the last twelve hours slammed shut behind the two men.

"Isaiah, I–"

He closed his mouth when Isaiah held up his hand.

"Not here."

Those were the first words his brother had spoken. Ian figured it was best not to say anything until ordered. Although he was the same age as his brother and two sisters, Isabella and Ivy, completing the set of Noble quadruplets, everyone knew Isaiah was the leader of their pack.

Rather than going out the front of the police station, Ian followed Isaiah through a back door that led to an alley, where a car was waiting.

Once they were inside the car, Isaiah started it and began to drive off.

After a few minutes, Ian looked over to his brother, whose fists were clenching the steering wheel.

"I'm used to you getting yourself into some sticky shit," Isaiah said. He shook his head. "But this...Ian, what the fuck?"

Ian had gained the reputation of being the latest bad boy chef working at one of the top restaurants in Las Vegas, but even this was a new low for him. But he was still determined to speak his peace.

"Look man, I swear...I had no clue that woman was married!"

Ian Noble could count on one hand the number of women who intimidated him...with one finger to spare. His mother, his sisters when they were pissed, and the woman boring a hole in the decorative rug between his couch and coffee table.

He turned and gave his brother a sidelong glance, which Isaiah ignored, then turned back to the woman.

"I thought you were on tour with Laurel."

The formidable Michelle Drake stopped, did her signature pivot on her sky-high heels causing her long slicked back pony-tail to whip over her shoulder, and looked up from the cell phone that was glued to her hands. Her brows pinched as her gaze landed on him.

"Laurel's tour ended two weeks ago and you know that."

Ian *did* know that, he was just trying to deflect for a moment. In fact, he was very aware that Laurel, her husband Rowan and Michelle were in Vegas on business at the same time Ian had gotten into his...altercation. Though Michelle didn't discuss her other client's business, Laurel Hunter had made it well known, in the couple of years that she'd been married to Rowan, that she was eager to slow down on touring, maybe even start a family. Getting an extended contract to headline a venue would possibly help to make that dream a reality. And what better place to do that than Vegas?

"I was supposed get on a plane this morning, that would take me to a white, sandy beach for my vacation," his publicist/manager said through clenched teeth, as she stormed in his direction. Another fact Ian had been well aware of, which was why he'd asked her a question he knew the answer to. "Instead, I'm here."

"Did he call you here?" Ian asked, tossing his head in the direction of his brother, who'd remained quiet. He'd already explained the previous night's events before to his brother.

Michelle gave him a mocking laugh. "Oh no." She clicked on her phone and Ian's TV caught his eye. Michelle had synced her phone to the digital media player connected to the TV and had the mirror setting on, allowing him to see everything she was looking at on her phone.

He didn't want to see what she was showing him, which

was a screenshot of one of the sleazy entertainment news websites.

"*MTZ*..." Michelle said, before swiping her finger across her phone to reveal screenshot after screenshot. "*GTV*... *Tonight's Entertainment*...MyScreen! My phone blowing up at one in the goddamned morning is what called me here!"

"Chelle–"

"Don't 'Chelle' me, Ian Noble," she said, closing her phone. She stepped right in front of him. "You are supposed to be on Your...Best...Behavior! The networks are watching you, making sure this 'bad boy' rep you've got is not out of control."

"It's not," Ian said.

"You sure as shit gave them a show last night." She jabbed her stiletto-shaped fingernail into his chest. "You better give me a good damn reason why I'm here, trying to save your behind rather than having mine planted in a beach chair with a daiquiri in my hand, or I swear I will shove this Louboutin *so* far up your ass that when you open your mouth, the only thing people will see is the red-bottom of my shoe."

Ian took a step back and rubbed his chest where Michelle had poked him with her sharp nails. He knew to shoot straight with her, because she was a beast at her job and if anyone could spin this whole ordeal in his favor, she could.

"A few weeks ago, I met a woman at the restaurant," he started.

Michelle rolled her eyes. "Of course you did."

"She was there on a weekend getaway with her girlfriends."

"How does this relate to last night?" Michelle asked.

Ian ran his hand over his low cut hair, down to his neck, where he felt tension building.

"It turns out, the guy who showed up at the restaurant bar after my shift was over...was her husband."

A string of obscenities flew from Michelle's lips.

After having a rough day, Ian had clocked out of work at

the restaurant and went to the bar for a drink. He'd been a bit tipsy when a strange man caught him off guard by yanking him around to introduce his fist to Ian's face. The man then caught Ian by the lapels of his unbuttoned chef's coat and harshly whispered that Ian had slept with his wife.

When Ian finally gathered his wits, he shoved the man away. If he'd been a bit more sober, he would have chosen his words more wisely. Instead, Ian had told the man that he had no idea who his wife was, but if she had to fly all the way to Vegas for a good time, then maybe he needed to step his game up.

After Ian's smart ass remark, chaos ensued; all of which was caught on camera.

"Okay," Michelle said, rubbing her forehead as she began to pace Ian's living room again. "The good news is he threw the first few punches, so it could appear like you were defending yourself."

"I *was* defending myself, Chelle," Ian argued, sitting down in one of his living room chairs.

"And your conversation couldn't be heard on any of the videos, so no one knows *what* the fight was about," she said, tossing him a look of censure. "But that doesn't mean this man won't try and go to the press and smear your name."

"Wouldn't be the first time," Ian murmured.

He'd had his close calls with women he'd met in the past trying to sell stories of their escapades to the media.

"Exactly," Michelle said. "Which is why we have to get ahead of this situation."

"And how do you propose we do that?"

"You need to go off the grid."

"What?!" Ian shouted, as he shot up out of his chair.

"You've, once again, brought too much attention to yourself. I'll do what I can on my end as far as damage control, but you need to let *me* do all the talking for you. You need to disappear and let this scandal die down."

"Chelle–"

"She's right."

Both Michelle and Ian turned to Isaiah, who'd spoken for the first time since they'd arrived at Ian's place.

"You need to lay low for a while," Isaiah said, quietly.

Michelle's phone rang and she stepped out of the room to take the call.

"Isaiah–"

Isaiah held up his hand and Ian shut his mouth.

"Look, I understand the situation. But what's done is done. And whether you knew it or not, the fact remains; you slept with a man's wife, Ian. Even if we can prevent that fact from getting out to the public, the fight is already all over the media and you're going to get backlash from it."

"You're already getting backlash from it," Michelle said, returning to the living room. She held up her phone. "That was the restaurant."

"What did they say?" Ian asked, feeling a sense of dread.

"Well...you're not fired," Michelle said.

Ian blew out a breath of relief.

"However..."

Shit.

"'However', what?" he asked.

"While you're not fired, they have decided to suspend you...without pay."

Ian felt like he wanted to put his fist through something. Preferably the bastard who'd caused all of this. Though with a more level head, he couldn't fault the man for coming after him. Had Ian had any inkling that the woman was married, he wouldn't have slept with her. Yes, he had a reputation for being a ladies' man, but even he had lines he didn't cross.

Ian ran his hands down his face.

"How long?" he asked.

"Ninety days."

His eyes bugged out as he looked at Michelle.

"As in...three months?"

"Yes. It's plenty of time for us to get this cleaned up."

"What...what the fuck am I supposed to do for three months?"

Chapter Two

"You come home to Sweet Rapids and work for Noble Naturals," Isaiah suggested.

Noble Naturals was their family's natural hair care business. They were now in the process of expanding the company to include bath, body and makeup products.

"That's a good idea," Michelle agreed, with a nod of her head. "You can finally put that other college degree of yours to good use."

Ian and his siblings, Isaiah, Isabella and Ivy were known in their hometown of Sweet Rapids, Nevada as the 'Noble Quads'. In their youth, they'd made headlines for being young geniuses and musical prodigies. Isaiah played the violin, Isabella played the harp, and Ivy played the bass violin. Ian's instrument of choice was the acoustic guitar.

The four of them graduated high school at fifteen and had their bachelor's degrees by eighteen.

While their father, the late Isaac Noble, had always wanted them to work for Noble Naturals, Ian and his siblings had chosen to minor in business to appease him, but majored in subjects that they were passionate about. Ian happened to have two passions: food and chemistry. So he'd double majored in culinary science and chemistry.

Isaiah had returned home to Sweet Rapids over a year ago, when another hair care line, Chic and Sleek, had decided to come out with their own natural line. Isaac Noble had summoned Isaiah home to figure out a way to retaliate. It was Isaiah's idea to expand Noble Naturals beyond natural hair care products.

Ian had told Isaiah he would help in any way he could with creating the new products, and apparently, Isaiah was finally cashing in on Ian's offer.

Ian was silent for several moments, thinking about what Isaiah had suggested.

"We've started on some of the products, but it would help to have another set of hands on deck."

"Are they screwing things up?" Ian asked.

Isaiah shook his head. "No one's screwing anything up, Ian. Giselle Warren has done a great job. It would just be nice if she had some more help. Some of the ideas she's working to put together are yours, after all."

Isaiah had a point. It had been a while since he'd focused on anything but food, and he felt like creating the products for Noble Naturals was a lot like cooking. There were recipes and you had to mix things just right to get the perfect results.

"Fine," Ian said, finally agreeing. "I'll come home until this...situation blows over."

"Good," Michelle said. "I'll make your travels arrangements. And once I put out a statement, I'm off to my vacation."

"Yeah, about that. I'm sorry, Chelle."

"You'll be much more sorry when you see my bill," she said, heading for the door. "Stay out of trouble!"

After Michelle was gone, Ian headed to the kitchen.

"I'm sure Mom's going to be excited. It feels like it's been too long since I've been home anyway."

"Especially considering you're only an hour or so away by plane," Isaiah murmured.

Sweet Rapids was located in Northwest Nevada, about thirty minutes south of Reno.

Ian pulled two bottles of water out of the fridge and looked around. He'd probably put his Vegas house up for rent. It made the most sense, especially since he'd be staying at his house in Sweet Rapids.

He tossed a bottle to Isaiah before he said, "I know we agreed to visit home more often, but it's been hard going back there and–"

"Dad's not there," Isaiah finished.

When Ian nodded, Isaiah did as well. "It's been nearly a year and I still feel like when I go to the house, I'll find him in his office working."

Their father had suffered a heart attack and he died on the operating table when he went in for bypass surgery. It had shattered the entire Noble family. Ian would never forget the look of pain on his mother and sisters' faces when the doctor came out to deliver the news. Ian had tried his best to be strong for the women in his family, but it was really Isaiah who held them all together, Ian concluded.

"It must be weird working in his old office then," Ian thought.

Isaiah had slowly begun to take over Noble Naturals over the last year. At first, he'd just been helping their mother, Irene, run the company. But she was slowly backing away from the company, giving Isaiah more responsibilities.

It had been no surprise that their father had requested Isaiah be his successor of Noble Naturals; since he was unspoken the leader of the four of them.

"It is," Isaiah admitted. "But it's also kind of comforting. I can feel his presence there."

"I'm not sure if that's a blessing or a curse," Ian teased, gaining a chuckle out of Isaiah. His brother had finally seemed to cool off after having to bail Ian out of jail.

"Sometimes it's both."

"How's Tessa?" Ian asked about Isaiah's girlfriend. They'd been dating over a year now.

"She's good," Isaiah said.

"And how's the bakery?"

Tessa and her sister, Dana, ran Everetts' Bakery in Sweet Rapids.

Ian noticed the way his brother's face brightened with pride. "The bakery is doing really well. Of course, you know they were featured on that travel cooking show. By the way, Tess can't stop thanking you for dropping a bug in the host's ear to visit their bakery."

Ian shrugged off the acknowledgement. He'd known the host of the show for years and had run into him after a meeting to discuss his own TV show. He'd casually mentioned the bakery and the next thing he knew, he was watching Tessa and Dana on TV.

"They've finally decided on a location for a second bakery," Isaiah said. "They plan on opening in a few months."

"Really?" Ian said, genuinely excited. Isaiah had once told Ian that it had always been a dream of Tessa and Dana's to open a second location, but their mother had been against it for a long time. Once Janet and Emmett Everett finally retired, she'd given them their blessing to run Everetts' Bakery as they saw fit, including opening more bakeries if they chose to.

"Yeah," Isaiah said. "Tess has been working her ass off, but I know it's going to pay off."

"And the two of you..." Ian pointed at him. "You guys are still good?"

"Oh yeah," Isaiah said. "Never better. In fact, I'm planning on proposing soon."

"No shit?" Ian said, a smile blooming on his face.

"We've been together over a year. She's practically moved in with me. And, of course, I love her like crazy. I can't imagine spending my life without her."

Ian came around the island and pulled his brother into a strong embrace.

"Congrats man! I'm happy for you."

Isaiah patted Ian on the back before pulling away.

"Thanks. Dana is helping me pick out a ring for her."

"When are you going to propose?"

"I haven't figured it out yet."

Ian knew that whenever Isaiah proposed, it would be nice that he was in Sweet Rapids to celebrate with his family. Maybe going home would be easier than he thought.

Giselle Warren bit into her sandwich as her lunch companion and co-worker, Thomas Walsh, shook his head and set his tablet down.

"That Ian Noble is forever getting in trouble."

Giselle looked up at Thomas and saw the way his brow was scrunched up. She glanced down at his tablet and noticed the *MTZ* video he had pulled up of Ian Noble throwing blows with an unidentified man.

"Looks like he was defending himself," she murmured before taking another bite of her sandwich.

"You're taking up for him?" Thomas asked, his eyes growing wide.

Giselle shook her head, causing her long black braids with purple highlights to sway from side to side.

"I don't *know* him well enough to defend him. I'm just saying what it looks like to me."

Giselle was a Sweet Rapids transplant, after attending the University of Nevada in Reno. She'd had one dream: to work for Noble Naturals. She'd been over the moon when they hired her and over the years, she'd worked her way up. And now, she was up for a promotion to head the Production Department that was creating new products for the company's expansion. Isaiah Noble had already told her she was shoe in.

She'd never met his brother, Ian, but she'd heard enough about him to know he had a reputation. But from what she'd heard, he'd toned down his wild ways in the last few years, or they weren't as publicized as they used to be anyway.

"Well *I* know him," Thomas said, seeming agitated. "And a bar brawl is right up his alley."

"All I'm saying is we don't know the entire story. I don't know why you even go to sites like *MTZ*."

"Because they always have the news before anyone else."

"Sometimes their wrong," she stated.

"They're rarely wrong. Anyway," Thomas continued. "Word on the street is Ian is coming home for a while."

"What's wrong with that?" Giselle asked as they finished their lunch.

"Everything. Trouble follows Ian Noble," Thomas said, with a warning.

He couldn't be that bad, Giselle thought. He came from a good family. So he'd gotten in some trouble and went to jail a few times. She'd spent a night or two behind bars before she cleaned up her act. And like she'd told Thomas before, Ian looked like he was defending himself and they didn't know the entire story.

What's the worst that could happen?

"This was nice."

Giselle looked up and gave Thomas a polite smile. "Yes, it was."

"Maybe we could finally try sharing a meal, outside of

work hours."

He was hinting at a date...again. Thomas was sweet, but she just wasn't attracted to him that way. Giselle wanted someone who made her heart race.

Kind of like it did when you were watching that video of Ian Noble?

Giselle stopped dead in her tracks.

Where had *that* thought come from?

She saw Isaiah every day, he had the same damn face as Ian, but she didn't react to him the way she'd reacted to that video of Ian.

Then again, she always had a thing for 'bad boys'. But she didn't fool with that type anymore, they were way too much trouble (and one of the reasons she'd spent a night or two in jail). But she also didn't fool with Thomas' type either.

Which reminded her, he was still waiting on an answer to his invitation. She went to her generic answer for whenever he tried to ask her out.

"Thomas, sharing lunch together is one thing. But I feel like anything more than that would be inappropriate."

"Because you don't date co-workers."

It wasn't exactly true...but it was a convenient enough excuse.

Giselle nodded. "Plus you know I occasionally work nights too." It was usually only once a month if that. But Thomas didn't need to know that.

Thomas shook his head and did a terrible job at masking his disgust. "I don't see how you can work at a place like that Giselle."

"Because it's fun and I enjoy myself. You're welcome to come and check it out sometime."

"I'll pass."

Giselle shrugged her shoulders and they stood and threw their trash away.

Lunch was over and they needed to get back to work.

Chapter Three

Ian pulled up to his mother's house the next morning and found Irene sitting on the porch with an expectant guise on her face. She was anticipating his arrival. It was obvious by the two mugs of coffee sitting next to a plate of bear claws.

She stood as he got out of his car and walked to the edge of the porch. He was quiet as he approached his mother and for some reason he felt the same way he'd felt as a child when he'd gotten in trouble and had to face her.

He climbed the steps and stopped when he and Irene were eye level.

"Hey, Mom."

The impassive look on her face morphed into a bright smile as she wrapped her arms around Ian. A breath he didn't realize he'd been holding fluttered from his lips and Irene chuckled.

"Boy, you looked like you did when you were little and about to get your butt whooped."

Ian laughed quietly. "That's how I *felt*."

Irene turned and went to her rocking chair and Ian sat in the one across from her.

"Nothing you do surprises me anymore, Ian."

Ian wasn't sure how he felt about his mother's comment.

"I have to admit," she added. "I'm not pleased with the circumstance that got you here. But I'm glad you're here."

She grabbed a bear claw off of the plate and Ian did the same.

"These from Everetts?"

"Mmm hmm," she said as she finished chewing. "Tessa brought a fresh batch over. She's such a sweet girl."

Ian nodded, agreeing with his mother. Tessa was a great woman and Isaiah had lucked up with her.

"I just wish Isaiah would hurry up and ask her to marry him. It *has* been over a year."

"He's been working hard with the company, as well as his own projects," Ian said, in defense of his brother.

"That's true," Irene conceded. "He's been doing so well. The transition from your father to Isaiah has been almost seamless."

Ian noticed the way his mother's smile dimmed a little and he felt the same wave of sadness wash over him at the thought of his father.

"How are you, Mom?"

Irene looked up at Ian and smiled. "Good days and bad days," she simply said. "Today is a good day. Having both of my boys back home. Now if I could only get your sisters here."

"Careful," Ian teased. "You're gonna start sounding like Dad plotting to get everyone home."

Irene covered her mouth and then laughed. "Oh I do, don't I? And all of those years I used to tell him not to bother the four of you. I know the girls will come back when it's their time. Isaiah did, and now you."

He didn't have the heart to tell her that he'd only be there for about three months and when his suspension was lifted, he was heading back to Vegas.

"How's your place here in Sweet Rapids?" Irene asked.

Ian smiled. "It's great, thanks to you and the groundskeeper."

Irene waved her hand. "I always had ulterior motives for watching your place," she said with a wink.

Ian laughed. "You know you're welcome to anything there."

"Oh I know. I took full advantage."

Ian laughed again. "Good."

"So," Irene said, before taking another bite of her bear claw. "When do you think your brother's going to pop the question?"

Ian picked up his coffee mug. He didn't know how much Isaiah had told Irene about his plans, so he tried to stay vague. Shrugging, he said, "Considering they've been practically living together for the last six months or so, probably sooner than later."

"The sooner they get married, the sooner they can get to work on my grandkids," Irene harrumphed.

Ian grinned at his mother as he took a sip of his coffee. It was exactly the way he liked it.

"You know," Irene said, in what appeared to be a casual tone, but Ian knew better. "If you settled down, found yourself a nice girl like Tessa, you wouldn't be caught up in some kind of trouble behind a woman all of the time."

Ian nearly choked on his coffee.

"You okay, baby?" Irene asked innocently, though her lip quirked up.

"I'm fine, Mom," he said after clearing his throat. "First of all, I don't usually have these types of problems with women."

"All it takes is one time and one woman to destroy you. Look at you, back at home on suspension from your job behind one."

He couldn't argue with his mother about that.

"Secondly," he continued. "Tessa is great and all, but when I do settle down, it won't be with someone like her."

"*When* you settle down?"

Ian blinked and looked at his mother. "Excuse me."

She had a wide grin on her face. "You said when."

Ian shook his head. "No, I said if."

"Ian Noble, don't tell me what I heard. I'm not *that* old. My hearing hasn't gone out on me yet. You said *when*."

Ian replayed the last bit of their conversation back in his mind.

Shit...

He did say when.

But that didn't mean anything...right?

"What type of woman *would* you settle down with?"

"Mom," Ian said, trying not to whine.

"Don't 'Mom' me in that tone, boy. *You* said when, not me. Now, humor me."

Ian sighed and sat back in the chair, stretching his legs out in front of him, staring off in the distance at the perfectly manicured lawn before them.

"She'd have to be engaging," Ian said. "Someone who can keep me on my toes."

"In other words, she'd have to be like you."

"Isn't that what 'finding the one' stuff is all about? Finding your equal?"

Irene nodded. "That's part of it," she said thoughtfully.

Ian sat in silence, waiting for his mother to elaborate. Instead, she changed the subject, asking, "When are you going in to the office?"

"I'll probably chill out for the weekend and then start fresh on Monday."

Irene nodded, smiling proudly. "You always did enjoy those chemistry sets when you were little."

"I suppose it will be nice to take a break from the kitchen and hang out in a lab for a while."

Ian sat with his mother for a while longer talking; the entire time his mind kept drifting back to his mother's words, 'That's part of it'.

He'd never been too curious before, but now he wondered, what else was there to finding the 'perfect match'?

"Are you gonna keep sitting there squirming or are you gonna tell me what's going on in that head of yours?"

Ian turned and looked at Isaiah, who was sitting on the other end of the couch, with eyes on the basketball game they were watching.

Well, Isaiah was watching. Ian's head had been all twisted up since his talk with their mother earlier.

There was no need to be uncomfortable where Isaiah was concerned, but still, this was new territory for him. Not that he really planned on exploring it, but he was still curious.

He tipped the beer in his hand back, took a long drag then blew out a breath before he spoke.

"How did you know Tessa was the one for you?"

That drew Isaiah's eyes away from the television.

"What?"

Ian shrugged. "You know, man. What was it about her that made you realize she was it for you?"

Isaiah sat back against the couch and leaned his head back.

"There was never just *one* thing," Isaiah said. "It's the total sum of her. Her smile, the way she walks, talks, her intelligence, and her drive. She has a quiet spirit that knows how to get just loud enough when necessary. I loved every aspect of her, even her flaws, like the way she has a habit of overthinking sometimes and freaking out." He smiled at the last comment.

"It's all of those things together that eventually made me realize, I couldn't imagine life without her. And I distinctly recall you also telling me not to fuck things up with her."

Ian chuckled, remembering that conversation.

"Where's all this coming from, Ian?"

Ian shook his head. "It's nothing. I was talking to Mom this morning and we were talking about Tessa. Of course, she said I should settle down with a nice woman like her and I said when I do, it wouldn't be with someone like Tessa. No offense."

"None taken," Isaiah said. "But...you said 'when'?"

Why the hell was everyone catching on to that one little word.

Ian scratched the back of his neck. "Mom caught the same thing. It was a slip. I didn't even realize I'd said it. I thought I said 'if'."

"But you said 'when'?" Isaiah reiterated.

"Yes," Ian said, annoyed. "What's the big damn deal?"

"The big deal," Isaiah said thoughtfully, "Is you've never said words that were linked to permanence when it came to the future and relationships."

Ian listened to his brother elaborate.

"With your careers, it was 'when I do this' or 'when I do that'. But with women, it's *always* been 'if I ever', never when."

"So what? You think me saying 'when' instead of 'if' this time was some kind of Freudian slip or something?"

Isaiah shrugged and stood. "I'm not saying anything man. But if that's what you think..." He went and threw his beer bottle away. "I've got to get out of here. Tessa and I are going out for Mediterranean by my place. You want to join us?"

The idea of having some of that delicious food was tempting. Being a third wheel, watching Tessa and Isaiah being all lovey-dovey, not so much.

"I'll pass, but thanks for the offer. Send Tessa my love."

Isaiah nodded and took off.

Once his brother was gone, Ian looked around.

It was Saturday night, and for the first time in ages, he was dateless.

Shaking his head, Ian snatched up his car keys and headed for the door.

Chapter Four

Ian sat back in the smoky burlesque club, sipping on his drink and enjoying the sights. After his brother had left, he knew he couldn't stay in the house. He knew damn well to stay away from a typical club. The last thing he needed was to hook up with another woman who'd get him into more trouble.

So he'd driven to Carson City to Joie de Burlesque. He'd been there a few times and enjoyed the performances the women put on. It wasn't like a strip club, where the women just took it all off for money. Here, the women told stories with their bodies; they teased and tantalized.

Ian was watching the last performer as she exited the stage, the tassels on her large breasts swinging around in opposite directions when the waitress brought him a refill.

"I hope you enjoyed Lady Susan," the emcee said, coming on stage. Ian joined the audience in giving the last performer a round of applause.

"Our next performer is a well-loved guest here at Joie de Burlesque. She doesn't perform often, but when she does, she shuts the house down."

Ian looked around as the crowd began to cheer even louder.

"Ladies and gentlemen, give it up for Gypsy!"

The lights dimmed, shrouding the club in nearly complete darkness and the sound of the curtain being opened could be heard. Ian sat up in his seat when the white wall behind the staged lit up in a red glow.

But what caught Ian's eye was the woman, Gypsy. She hung from an aerial silk hammock, as it slowly spun in circles. Her head was back, neck resting on part of the fabric while one leg was sexily crossed over the other. Her arms dangled loosely beneath her until the music began.

One arm glided above her, her hand sliding up the silk to grab it. Her legs uncrossed and her body leaned back until she was upside down, being held up by only the silk wrapped around one leg.

Ian watched, mesmerized by the grace and strength Gypsy possessed as she intertwined her body in every direction imaginable. He actually found himself shifting in his seat when he watched her stretch out flat against the bottom of the hammock and roll her entire body provocatively against the fabric. His mind drifted to what it would feel like to be beneath her, to feel her doing those same movements, rolling her body on top of his.

There was something intriguing about watching Gypsy's performance while unable to see her face. The only light on stage was the red wall behind her, so only her silhouette was visible.

But damn...what a silhouette!

Everything about her body screamed sensuality as she continued her performance. She pulled her body up to stand, wrapped the silks around her arms and floated in the air, her legs suspended in a split. Then she hooked her legs around the silks several times and the audience let out a collective gasp when she released her arms and suddenly dropped, her body dangling upside.

The crowd applauded as she lifted herself up again, untangled her feet and ended her performance in the same pose she'd began in. The red light dimmed and the curtain closed, while the audience applauded.

Once the applause died down, Ian paid for his drinks, stood and headed to the back.

"Noble!" Frank, the owner of the club, and the man Ian had been searching for, said. "You're a sight for sore eyes."

Ian shook Frank's hand before being pulled into a welcoming embrace.

"How you doin', Frank?" Ian asked. "The place still looks good."

"Yeah, well, can't complain," he said. "You enjoy the show?"

"No doubt," Ian said. "I see you added some new things."

"Oh you mean Gypsy," Frank said, grinning before nudging an elbow in Ian's side. "You like her, huh? Yeah, GiGi's good people. Comes in about once a month or so to perform."

"It was impressive," Ian said. "But different than the other performances."

"It is. But the crowd loves her. I'd love to stay and chat, but I've got another performer to announce. We've got to catch up soon."

"Of course. Before you take off, is there any chance of me getting to meet–"

Frank held up his hand. "Sorry man, no can do. GiGi likes her privacy on show nights."

All Ian could do was nod. He had to respect the woman's wishes. "I understand."

"But she'll be back in a month," Frank said with a wink.

Ian would still be in Sweet Rapids then. And between now

and then, he was determined to figure out who Gypsy really was.

"I'll see you then."

The silk hammock lowered and Giselle's feet hit the stage floor. She headed toward the wings of the stage and one of the stagehands held a robe open for her. She slid her arms in and turned tying the belt tightly around her waist before taking the water the stagehand was holding for her as well.

She thanked him and then made her way to her dressing room. Several women complimented her on her performance as she walked by. When Giselle arrived at her dressing room, she sat down at her vanity.

Her adrenaline was still pumping. She always got a rush from performing in front of the crowd. It was such a switch from her day job as a chemist, but to her, the aerial silks were a form a release.

She'd just finished changing out of costume and back into her regular clothes when she heard a knock at the door.

"Come in," she offered.

Frank poked his head in a smiled.

"Another great performance!" Frank said, clapping his hands.

"Aww, thanks Frank. And thank you for penciling me in on short notice. I know I wasn't officially on the schedule until next month."

"Hey, Joie de Burlesque is your home as far as I'm concerned. Next month's show with you as the feature is almost sold out already. If you ever decide you want to quit your day job, you've got a permanent spot here."

Frank had been giving Giselle that offer for a long time now.

"There are a lot more talented women that deserve top billing than me," Giselle said. "Besides, I don't think I'd ever quit my day job. I love science and Noble Naturals too much. And I told you, I'm up for a promotion."

"Well the offer still stands. You always wow the crowd. In fact..." Frank chuckled. "It seems you had a new admirer in the crowd tonight."

"Really?" Giselle said, grinning.

"Yep, even wanted to meet you after the performance. But I let him know that you demanded privacy."

"Thank you, Frank."

"But he'll be back next month, he said," Frank informed her. He turned and headed for the door. "You have a good night, GiGi."

Giselle said good night as well. Curious, she asked, "Who was the guy?"

"Noble," Frank said.

Giselle's brow furrowed. "Isaiah and Tessa have seen me perform several times."

Frank shook his head. "Not Isaiah. Ian Noble."

After Frank left the room, Giselle dropped down into her seat. Ian Noble had been in the crowd?

And he'd wanted to see her afterward?

Suddenly her mouth felt dry and she licked her lips, the ball of her tongue ring scrapping her lip.

"Holy shit," she whispered.

Chapter Five

Giselle arrived at Noble Naturals early Monday morning. That was nothing new lately with the company prepping to roll out the first round of new products to the test groups soon. She wasn't naive enough to believe that all of the products would be a hit on the first go around but that didn't mean she wasn't going to try.

And she wanted to prove to Isaiah that she deserved the Head of Production promotion.

Another reason she was up early was because of the thoughts of Isaiah's brother that had plagued her all night. She'd barely gotten any sleep over the last couple of nights.

She'd already been off kilter since her lunch with Thomas, when he'd shown her the video of Ian's fight and she'd been strangely turned on, but then to find out that Ian had been at Joie de Burlesque and watched her perform and enjoyed it...

Giselle got off of the elevator on her floor and walked down the quiet hallway to the lab. Her eyebrow raised when she noticed that the hook where Thomas usually kept his coat was empty. After grabbing her own, she slid her arms into the sleeves as she entered the lab.

"Thomas," she said, cheerfully, as she buttoned her lab coat. "You're here early."

She was ready to get to work and hopefully get the irrational crush on a man she'd never even met out of her mind.

She was still walking toward him when he stood to his full height, causing Giselle to nearly stumble.

Thomas wasn't that tall.

Who in the world...

The air rushed from her lungs when the man turned around and locked eyes with hers.

Ian Noble.

"Who's been screwing with my formula?"

Giselle blinked, coming out of her trance.

"Excuse me?"

Ian turned and picked up a piece of paper.

"My formula," he repeated. "Somebody changed some of the components to it."

"Oh...uh...I did," she said.

"And who are you?"

"I'm Giselle Warren."

Ian's head tilted to the side as he studied her for a moment.

"*You're* Giselle Warren?"

Giselle's eyes widened. Her braids were pulled up on the top of her head in a bun to avoid any mishaps in the lab, she had a tiny diamond stud in her nose and the balls of her tongue ring were blue today to match her blouse.

She stood up straight and squared her shoulders as she glared at him. That crush she'd had a minute ago, was quickly dissipating.

"Yes," she said, through clenched teeth. "I'm Giselle Warren, and I don't think I like your tone right now, Mr. Noble."

"So you know who I am."

"You're reputation precedes you."

That seemed to be like a slap in the face because his face morphed quickly. He cleared his throat and looked away.

"Sorry, I didn't mean anything by it. You're just...my brother didn't describe you."

"What *did* he tell you about me?" she asked.

He looked at her again. "Just that you were good at your job."

"And that's all that matters," she said with a curt nod. She brushed past him and his masculine scent assaulted her scenes. Why did he have to smell so damn good? "Now if you'll excuse me, I'd like to get to work."

"Wait a second," Ian said. "Earlier, you said you were the one who changed this formula."

"Yes," she said, trying to ignore how close he was to her.

"Why?"

"There were too many ingredients."

"What?"

Giselle swallowed a sigh and turned to face him again. He was too damn close. She could feel his body heat and it was driving her crazy.

"There were too many ingredients," she repeated.

He looked down at the paper again and studied it. She watched, trying not to be intrigued by the way he pulled his lip between his teeth and his brow furrowed.

"I'll be damned," he finally said. He looked up at her and her treacherous knees buckled ever so slightly at the sight of his full smile. "I guess you're right."

"I know I'm right," Giselle said, confidently as she turned back around.

"I suppose I'll have to reevaluate some of my old notes," he murmured to her back.

"That might be wise."

"You're mad at me." There was a sense of wonder in his voice at his revelation.

"I'm not mad, Mr. Noble." She was kinda mad.

"Please, call me Ian."

"Ian..." Damn that sounded too good. "I'm not mad."

"Giselle..."

She bit the inside of her cheek to keep from moaning at the sound of Ian saying her name. She didn't like him...she didn't like him...she didn't like–

"I'd like for us to get along while I'm running things here."

Giselle whirled back around, and her eyebrows shot up.

"Running what?" she asked.

"Running the Production Department, of course. My brother hasn't officially announced it yet, but I'm here to help get these new products created."

Giselle felt the heat rise up her body and she felt like fire was going to shoot out of her ears.

"I don't think so," she said, storming past Ian.

Ian sat on the sofa watching as Giselle paced the length of Isaiah's office. The woman was livid. He decided it was best not to say anything more until his brother arrived. She looked like she would haul off and smack him at any moment.

He studied the four inch closed-toe booties she was stomping around in. Long, gorgeous, toned legs spilled from beneath her lab coat. Her dress or skirt was obviously shorter than the coat, so it made him imagine her with nothing on underneath.

Ian shook his head.

He was too horny for his own good. First Gypsy at Joie de Burlesque, now Giselle; whose legs reminded him of Gypsy's.

Speaking of Gypsy...

He'd spent the weekend scouring the internet for her with no success. It was like the woman was a damn ghost. His unfruitful search was also the reason for his sleepless night. When morning dawned, he decided he may as well come in early and get a peek at what the production team was working on and take notes so he could give his input.

He hadn't expected to run into Giselle Warren that early. And he *definitely* didn't expect her to be so damn...hot!

He figured she'd be an older woman, not...this.

His eyes roamed her body from head to toe. Her hair was up in those black and purple braids and a small portion of the sides and back of her head were shaved with intricate designs.

She had a piercing in that adorable nose of hers, and the balls of her barbell tongue ring were blue.

Yours are gonna be blue too if you don't get some soon.

He ran his hands down his face and stifled a groan.

"This is ridiculous."

Ian looked over his fingers and noticed Giselle was still pacing and now she was murmuring to herself. Suddenly, she turned to face him shooting daggers at him with her eyes.

"What is the problem, Giselle?"

He'd been confused as to why she'd taken off in a rage, but for some reason he found himself following her. She'd marched to the elevator, jabbed the up button and stood there tapping her foot impatiently until the doors slid open. She must not have realized he was behind her until she entered the elevator and turned around. Her eyes and grown wide before narrowing. She'd huffed, and then pushed the button to the floor where the executive suites were located and then pressed her body in the corner of the elevator as far away from him as possible.

"The 'problem' is you," Giselle said, snapping Ian back to the present.

"Me?" he asked. "How am I a problem?"

"You are a problem, popping up here, thinking you're going to be running things."

Ian chuckled and shook his head, stretching his arms across the back of the sofa. "You did see the name on the building when you walked in this morning, didn't you?"

"I don't give a flying fuck whose name is on this building," she spat out.

The smile on Ian's face faded away and he stood.

"Who the hell do you think you're talking to?" he asked, moving toward her. "You do realize I could have you fired."

She didn't even flinch. "You're here a whole two minutes and you think you can throw your weight around. Let me tell you something, Ian Noble. Your last name may be *on* the building, but I've made my mark *in* this company. You haven't been here, working your ass off day and night; I have. That Head of Production position is mine. I don't care who you are."

"I see you two have met already."

Both Ian and Giselle turned their heads to find Isaiah standing in the doorway. Ian locked eyes with his brother, who had an amused grin on his face. He turned and looked at Giselle and that's when he realized their bodies were practically pressed against one another.

Giselle was the first to back away. She turned to Isaiah, pointed at Ian and without preamble asked, "Is he the new Head of Production?"

Ian turned to face his brother as well, smug look on his face as he waited on Isaiah's response.

Isaiah blew out a breath, as look of remorse filled his face.

He's going to break it to her gentl–

"No."

Chapter Six

"No?"

Isaiah cleared his throat and looked toward Giselle. "Will you excuse us, Giselle?"

The smile of triumph radiated from her lips and made her entire body glow. As frustrated as he was at the moment, all he wanted to do was kiss that self-righteous look off of her face.

"Of course," Giselle said, before sauntering out of Isaiah's office.

Damn, her ass is sexy.

Ian shook his head, telling himself to focus, before turning back to his brother.

"No?" he repeated.

Isaiah sighed again and headed for his desk.

"It's too early for this shit."

"For you to betray your own brother?"

Isaiah sat down behind the desk that was once their father's.

"You keep those dramatics up and you're gonna start sounding like Izzy and Ivy," Isaiah said dryly.

"What the fuck was that all about?"

"That wasn't personal, Ian."

Ian blinked. "'Wasn't personal'? You do realize we're brothers, right? That sure as hell felt personal."

Isaiah folded his hands together and placed them on the desk.

Now, Ian was pacing the office.

"I can't believe you let her think I wasn't going to be running things. You made me look like a damn fool in front of her."

"I'm sure you did a bang up job of that all by yourself. And you're not running things, at least not in the way you think."

"This is our company! Dad would have–"

"Done the exact same thing," Isaiah said, cutting him off. "He was always a fair man. So stop acting like some entitled child over a job you barely wanted to begin with and sit down."

Ian stopped in his tracks and looked at Isaiah. It was rare moments like this when Isaiah flexed his muscles that, for a split second, Ian almost thought his brother was older by years rather than minutes.

As Ian sat back down on the sofa he'd occupied when Giselle was in the room with him, Isaiah continued. "Dad's dream was for us to come into the fold of the business, but he was no fool. He knew we had our own passions that had led us away from Noble Naturals and he, despite not fully liking the idea, understood that there was a chance that we would decide to continue with our career choices rather than working here. He had contingency plans. And Giselle Warren was one of those plans."

"But I'm here now," he argued.

"For three months, Ian," Isaiah reminded him. "Yes, I want your help while you're here. I'm grateful for it. But I have to think *past* those three months. Giselle has been here for years, she's *earned* the position, and I've promised it to her. While you're here, you will work with her and consult with her. But I can't go back on my word; the Head of Production job is hers."

Everything Isaiah was saying made perfect sense, especially since Ian planned to be on the first smoking thing out of Sweet Rapids once his suspension at the restaurant was up. His ultimate goal was his own cooking show, and he'd been so close before the fight. If he were honest, he didn't really want the head position anyway.

Giselle had just opened that mouth of hers and it had gotten under his skin.

"I wasn't thinking straight," Ian finally admitted.

"I wonder why," Isaiah said, unfolding his hands and leaning back in his chair.

"Shit," Ian whispered. "What am I supposed to do now?"

"You tuck your tail between your legs and you get to work."

By the time Giselle arrived back to the lab, the work day was officially beginning.

Thomas was in the lab, looking confused.

"Good morning," he said. "Uh...have you seen my lab coat?"

Giselle nodded.

"Yeah, it seems we've got someone new on board."

"Who?" Thomas asked, and then his face filled with disdain. "Noble!"

Giselle was taken aback by the way Thomas spewed the man's name. Yes, she was annoyed as hell by him at the moment, but Thomas' reaction was downright venomous.

"Yes," Giselle said, and then retold the events of the morning.

"I told you he was going to be nothing but trouble."

"If you have a problem with me, feel free to leave."

Giselle turned to find Ian standing behind them. The look on Ian's face held as much contempt as Thomas'.

"Noble," Thomas spat out.

"Walsh."

"Been a long time."

Ian rolled his eye and snorted. "Not long enough apparently."

Giselle's head bounced from one man to the other, as if she were watching a ping pong match.

"Giselle."

Why did her body have to react so strongly when this man said her name? She turned her attention to him. She wished she could have been a fly on the wall, listening in on the conversation between Ian and Isaiah.

"Yes?"

"May I speak to you?" Ian cut his eyes to Thomas, who was still glaring in their direction. "*Privately*?"

She gave Ian a slight nod, and she turned and led the way to one of the inner rooms of the lab. She turned and watched as Ian closed the door.

"I owe you an apology."

"Yes, you do."

He smiled and dammit if it didn't make her wet seeing that set of perfectly white, straight teeth...

"You don't make it easy, do you?"

She folded her arms across her chest and shrugged.

"The past two weeks have been absolute hell, and I barely got any sleep last night."

Not getting much sleep the night before, she understood, especially since he was the reason for her sleepless night.

"But none of that is an excuse for me to have been rude to you this morning," he added.

She studied him for a minute before asking, "How hard is it right now for you to admit you're wrong?"

"Considering I'm rarely wrong..." he teased.

She didn't want to be amused by him. She didn't want to like him, especially after the way they'd clashed this morning. But here he was, eating crow.

"My father taught me that when I'm wrong, I need to own up to my mistakes."

"Your father was a good man," Giselle said. "It's not the same around here without him."

"It's not the same anywhere without him," Ian said, somberly.

She could hear the sadness in his voice.

"Giselle, I'm sorry we got off to a bad start."

She looked into his eyes and knew he was being sincere.

"I apologize as well. I was also a bit rude to you in Isaiah's office."

"How hard is it for *you* to admit that?" he asked, with a grin.

Giselle fought the smile tugging at her lips, but Ian caught it.

"You were only speaking the truth," Ian said. "My brother says you've worked hard with Noble Naturals over the years, and my father thought so too. You've earned the position."

"Thank you," Giselle said. "Like you said earlier, I'd like for us to get along, while you're here."

"I'd like that too."

"I took some notes on some of the formulas for some of your products. There were a few I was having trouble getting right."

"I'm sure together we'll be able to figure it."

They stood there for a moment in an awkward silence.

"I...I guess we'd better get to work," Giselle said, before

heading toward the door. As soon as she returned to her lab table, Thomas was at her side.

"Are you okay?"

"Yes, Thomas, I'm fine."

"Then why do you look so flustered?"

Because Ian Noble is too fine for his own good. There was a hint of electricity in the room before Giselle had broken eye contact.

"What did he say to you?" Thomas demanded.

Giselle tried not to be annoyed by Thomas' questioning. He almost sounded like a jealous boyfriend. "We cleared the air. He apologized, and so did I. End of story. We'd like to attempt to have an amicable interaction while he's helping us out."

"We don't need his help."

"A lot of these formulas for the soaps and lotions *are* his."

"You're defending him again."

"I'm stating a simple fact, Thomas," she said, keeping her voice low. Ian had made his way over to another table on the other side of the lab. He was chatting animatedly with a few of the other lab workers. She let out a sigh, before asking, "Can we please just get to work? We have a lot to do today."

"Are we still on for lunch?"

This was becoming a habit Giselle didn't want to entertain. She'd have to figure out a way to start letting him down gently. But since she'd already agreed today, she said, "Yes, we're still on for lunch."

Thomas, seeming satisfied with her answer, turned and headed for his own table. Giselle pulled her phone out of the pocket of her lab coat, unraveled the cord to her headphones, and stuck them in her ears. She found her 'Work Playlist' and turned it on.

She got into her natural groove of working, but after about half an hour, she could feel eyes on her. She looked up from the formula she was working on for a makeup foundation to find Ian staring at her.

He nodded his head, and then went back to work. She noticed he also had earbuds in his ears. From her peripheral, she felt Thomas' censorious glare. She looked from one man to the other and wondered...why did these two men seem to hate each other?

Chapter Seven

Ian looked up when he noticed Giselle leaving for lunch.

With Walsh.

Ian shook his head as Thomas placed his hand on the small of her back. When Giselle slid out of his grasp, a satisfied grin spread across Ian's face.

After they left the lab, he went back to work revising some of his formulas. Giselle had been right about some of them not needing as many ingredients. He hadn't even looked at them since he'd created them in college; and he'd never tried any of them out.

Though he missed cooking, he had to admit, he was going to enjoy creating these new products for Noble Naturals.

"Hey."

Ian looked up and saw Isaiah coming toward his lab table.

"Hey man," Ian said, before looking back down at his old notebook.

"Have you eaten yet?"

Ian shook his head, reading over Giselle's sticky notes. "Nah."

"Take a break," Isaiah said. "Come have lunch with me."

Ian pinched the bridge of his nose as he closed his fatigued eyes. "Sure, I could use a break, I guess."

Rather than leaving the facility, they decided to head for the company cafeteria.

Isaiah went for a chicken salad, while Ian picked up the soup of the day.

"So, did you apologize to Giselle?"

Ian took a sip of soup, scrunched his nose up and grabbed the shakers on the table. He sprinkled a few different seasonings into the soup, tasted it again and then nodded his head in approval.

"Of course I did."

"Good," Isaiah said, before digging into his salad.

"You never told me Wack-Ass-Walsh worked here."

"Oh yeah, I forgot you two had issues."

"*I* never had an issue with him."

"Yet you broke his nose."

"He had it coming," Ian murmured.

Isaiah sat his fork down and studied his brother. "Is this going to be a problem?"

"Not for me," Ian said with a shrug. "But I can already tell that Walsh isn't pleased with my presence."

"Maybe I should talk to him."

"About what?" Ian asked. "We're both adults. And that incident happened like what...ten years ago?"

"True, but you're supposed to be staying out of trouble."

"I'm not looking for trouble."

"Yet it always seems to find you."

"Look man, I plan to keep to myself as much as possible. Besides, Giselle is the Head of Production now, so anything I need to discuss, I can discuss with her."

"I bet."

"What does that mean?"

"You don't think I didn't notice the way you were checking her out when she left my office this morning."

There was no point in denying it, so he simply said, "She's an attractive woman."

"But...?" Isaiah asked.

"But," Ian added. "It seems like she might have something going on with Walsh."

"Really?" Isaiah asked, surprised and then shook his head. "I don't think so."

"He was definitely kind of touchy feely with her before they left for lunch together. She moved away, but that could have just been to keep up professional appearances."

He hoped she wasn't seeing Thomas. Not because the thought of her with him filled him with a possessiveness that made absolutely no sense whatsoever; but simply because Thomas Walsh was, in Ian's opinion, a fuckboy. And Ian had a feeling that Giselle Warren was much more woman than Thomas could handle.

Isaiah voiced Ian's thoughts out loud. "Giselle is too much woman for Thomas. I can't see her with a guy like him."

Ian shook his head. "Stranger things have happened," he said, before he went back to his soup.

"So Ian Noble just popped up in your lab acting like he was the big boss?"

Giselle laughed with her older sister, Ciara, who was on the phone.

"Yep," Giselle said. "And you should have seen his face when I asked his brother if he was making Ian Head of Production and he said no."

"I bet you were just tickled pink."

"Yes," Giselle admitted. "That's what he gets for coming in there strutting around like he's big shit."

"He *is* big shit, Giselle. He's part owner of the company. And you really said–"

"I didn't give a flying fuck whose name was on the building? Yes, I did."

"That's my GiGi," Ciara said, a smile in her voice. After a moment of silence, she sighed and asked, "How are you?"

"I'm fine, CiCi," Giselle said.

"Good. Sometimes I think you work too hard out there."

"You sound like Mom, with all of that worrying."

"I'm your big sister, it's my job. And speaking of Mom, she wants to know when you're coming out to the East Coast for a visit?"

Giselle sighed. She'd been meaning to make a trip to North Carolina, but time always got away from her.

"You guys know I'm swamped with work, especially since we're getting these products ready for the test groups."

"I know."

"You guys should come out here," Giselle insisted.

"You know I'd love to, but with Eddie and the baby–"

"I understand. I'll try to make it home when things slow down."

"Mom will be pleased to hear that."

"I'll give her a call soon."

"Shit, I gotta go, sis. The baby is crying."

"Go, and give my niece a big kiss from her Aunt GiGi. Tell Eddie I said hello."

"I will. I love you, honey," Ciara said.

"I love you too."

"Take care of yourself," her older sister ordered.

"Yes ma'am."

Giselle hung up her phone and set it down on the coffee table. She was glad to have checked in with her sister. They spoke a few times a week. Growing up, they'd been inseparable. Ciara had always been Giselle's lifeline.

Giselle thought back to their conversation and the topic of the evening, which happened to be Ian. He'd still been at work when she took off for the day. On this particular day, she taught an evening yoga class, otherwise she would probably still be would at work too. She'd been tempted to go back to work, but she felt tired after the class. So instead of going back to work, she was at home, with a nice merlot and a good book for the evening.

She wouldn't dare mention her fatigue to Ciara. She loved her sister, but she tended to be on the overprotective side. Especially since she'd had her baby. She'd have kept on fussing about Giselle working too hard.

After sitting and attempting to read for a while, she realized she was too distracted. Ian Noble once again filled her thoughts. Sighing, she grabbed the remote and flicked on her stereo. She scrolled through her phone until she found the song she was looking for and synced her phone with the stereo. She hit play and music filled her apartment.

She walked slowly to the corner of the room, where a silk hammock hung from the ceiling. She circled it a few times before reaching up with both hands to grab it and pull herself up.

She did a few intricate moves before stretching the hammock wide so she could lay in it. She stared out her window at the sky that was just beginning to darken, several stars dotting the sky.

She thought back on the events of the day. She'd gone into work early, because he'd been on her mind all night. And then, as if she'd conjured him up, he was there in the lab. Once they'd gotten past their initial meeting and called a truce, they worked in the lab for the majority of the day in silence.

She'd been attracted to the man before they'd even met. But now...

Giselle shook her head.

"It's *still* ridiculous," she told herself. "His time here is temporary. And you don't hook up with co-workers anyway."

Even she wasn't convinced by those words.

But convinced or not, she was not hooking up with Ian Noble.

No matter how strong the desire to was.

Chapter Eight

"Good morning, Giselle."

Giselle looked up and pulled an earbud out of her ear. Ian stood there, looking ridiculously handsome. He was wearing a light blue button down shirt, beneath a charcoal colored vest. The top few buttons were undone, showing off some of his chest. He wore a dark pair of jeans and finished the look off with a stylish pair of work boots.

This man is fine.

"Good morning," she finally replied.

"You all right?" he asked, one eyebrow hiking upward.

"I'm fine. How are you this morning?"

"I'm good. What are you working on?"

She looked down at the items in front of her. "A BB cream foundation."

"I have no clue what that is."

Giselle threw her head back and laughed. "That doesn't surprise me. None of the other men in here know either. Which is why I took it upon myself to focus on the makeup items with the other women."

Ian nodded and then held out a to-go cup to her.

"What is this?" she asked.

"Let's call it a peace offering."

She took the cup from him and tried not to tremble when his fingers brushed hers.

We had this discussion last night, her brain chastised. *Ian Noble is off limits.*

But that didn't stop the flutter in her belly when they locked eyes and she noticed a flicker of awareness in them. Did he feel that strange sensation between the two of them as well?

"Try it," he insisted.

She brought the cup to her lips, took a sip and sighed.

"Okay..." she said, shaking her head. "Where did you get this? This is the best coffee I've ever tasted."

"I'm glad you like it. It's my own special blend."

"You..." She looked down at the cup. "*You* made this yourself?"

She took another sip.

"You seem surprised," he said with a smile.

"I shouldn't be, all things considered. But...yeah, I am."

His smile widened. "You just may discover that I'm full of surprises."

"The only thing that would make this better is a pastry from–"

"Everetts'?"

Her eyes rounded when he finished her sentence.

"How? They're not even open yet."

"Well, when one of the owners is your future sister-in-law, you get a few perks." Ian held up a box. "How about we go and sit in the office?"

Giselle thought his suggestion was a good idea. "Let me take these gloves off and wash my hands. I'll meet you in there."

Ian reached out and took the coffee from her hand. She pulled the latex gloves off, tossed them in the trash and then went to wash her hands. By the time she reached the office, Ian had the coffees on the table and the pastry box open.

"After you," he insisted and she picked a large cinnamon roll out of the box before sitting in the chair behind the desk. Ian chose a blueberry muffin for himself and they began to eat.

She looked up and found him staring at her.

"What is it?" she asked. "Do I have something on my face?"

"What? No," Ian said. He looked around the room. "I was just thinking...you look good in here, behind this desk. My brother was right to give you the position."

"Thank you," she said, smiling at his compliment. His mention of Isaiah gave her a thought. "Earlier you called Tessa your future sister-in-law. Are she and Isaiah going to be making some kind of announcement soon?"

"Hmm," Ian said, finishing the food in his mouth. He wiped his hands on a napkin. "I guess I kind of let that slip a bit."

Giselle watched as he looked over his shoulder, then back at her.

"Just between you and me, I have it on good authority that Isaiah does plan on proposing soon."

"That's great. They are great together. It was only a matter of time before they got married."

"I agree. I can't think of a better woman for my brother."

They fell into silence for a while, as they continued eating their breakfast.

"So, what's the deal with you and Walsh?"

The question caught Giselle off guard and she nearly choked on a piece of cinnamon roll.

"Shit!" Ian said, jumping up from his seat as she coughed uncontrollably. "Giselle, are you okay?"

She held up her hand, nodding.

Ian picked up her cup of coffee. "Here, drink some."

She took the cup from him and took a sip as he soothingly rubbed her back. She wished he would stop. It felt so good.

"You good?" he asked.

"Yes."

He watched her for another minute before going back to the other side of the desk to his seat.

"Thomas and me?" she asked, then shook her head. "There is *nothing* going on between Thomas and me."

Ian held his hands up in defense. "It's none of my business, I know. I was just curious."

"I don't date co-workers."

She threw out her standard line, not just as a statement but as a reminder to herself, once again. Ian was now her co-worker, for however long he was going to be there. She figured if it worked with Thomas, it would work with him too.

But she wasn't as convinced as she usually was when she said those words.

"Understandable. Things can get messy getting involved with someone you work with."

"Yeah...messy."

"Well," Ian said, standing. "I better get to work."

"Right...work." As she watched Ian turn to leave the office, she called out to him. "Hey, thanks for the coffee and breakfast."

His lip quirked up and the hint of a dimple deepened his cheek.

"My pleasure."

Ian clicked a button on his computer screen to minimize the video he'd pulled up on MyScreen's website.

It wasn't Gypsy.

He'd watched the few videos Joie de Burlesque had posted

of her on their page, but he couldn't see her face. The video he'd just attempted to watch, unfortunately, wasn't Gypsy.

Even though he hadn't been able to see her face, the shape of her body was imprinted in his memory. There'd been several other performers who went by the name, but none of them had a body like *his* Gypsy's.

Giselle's body is like Gypsy's...

Ian tried to shake the thoughts of Giselle out of his head. His desire to figure out who Gypsy had waned in the month since he'd started working with Giselle. But he had to keep reminding himself that she was off limits.

Even though she denied that there was anything going on between them, Walsh seemed to always be sniffing around her.

Ian didn't like it one bit. But he also reminded himself that it was none of his business. Giselle was a grown woman, who could handle herself. And Walsh had never done anything that Ian felt the need to step in to intervene over.

He'd gone to Joie de Burlesque the night before to see Gypsy perform again to a sold out crowd, in an attempt to distract himself from thinking of Giselle; but this time as he watched her vigorous, yet sensual performance, he couldn't stop his mind from imagining what Giselle would look like up there on the silks.

Maybe he'd invite her to see Gypsy the next time she performed. Giselle seemed like the type to enj–

You can't ask her out, his brain yelled at him.

Ian sniffed and then looked up when he noticed smoke billowing over his head.

"Shit."

He hopped up from his seat, rushed to the stove and turned it off. He swore again as he looked down at the burnt pan of risotto.

He snatched the pan off of the stove, carried it to the sink and dumped the contents down the disposal before hitting the switch.

His best dish ruined. All because he couldn't stop thinking of a woman.

What the hell was going on with him?

Chapter Nine

"Dammit," Giselle cursed, slamming a plastic beaker down on the lab table.

"What's wrong?"

She jumped at the sound of Ian's voice behind her.

"You scared me half to death," she breathed.

"Sorry," he said as he headed back to his own table.

"I thought you were gone for the day," Giselle said.

Ian shook his head. "Nah, just needed a break. I got stuck on something. Looks like you are too."

Giselle blew out a frustrated breath and nodded. "Yeah, I can't figure out what's going wrong. This should be something simple."

"Bring it over with your notes," Ian said. "Maybe we can help each other out."

Giselle gathered her things and headed over toward Ian.

"What's going on?" he asked.

"It's this mud mask I've been working on. It's way too–"

"Soupy?" Ian asked, picking up the beaker and gently stirring it.

"Yes! It's soupy. Nobody's going to want to put this shit on their face."

"Hey," Ian said in a soothing tone. "Just take a deep breath. Like you said, it should be simple. You're probably just over-thinking. Here, take a look at this."

He picked up a mold and handed it to her.

"Open it," he said, when she took it from his hand.

She pulled open the mold and a crumbly mess fell out.

"My bath bombs aren't exactly coming out right either."

"You think?" she teased, wiping the dusty remnants out of her way. "It smells good though. What's in it?"

"Rose and patchouli."

"Why do you think it's falling apart?"

"I don't know," Ian said, rubbing his hand over his eyes. He was exhausted. "But how about we take a break from our own projects and look at each other's? Maybe they need fresh eyes."

"That sounds like a good idea."

They switched notes and studied them for a while.

"I think I've got an idea for your bath bomb," she finally said.

"Yeah?"

"Yeah, do you mind?" she asked, pointing at the items on the table.

"By all means," Ian said.

Giselle got to work creating a new bath bomb. Ian came around to the side of the table she was working on and stood over her shoulder.

"What are you doing differently?" he asked.

She could feel his breath on her shoulder. It sent chills down her spine.

"I...uh...I'm adding a bit of shea butter," she said. "It should help hold everything together."

She finished filling the mold and turned to face him. He didn't back up, so their bodies were incredibly close.

His mouth was moving, but she didn't catch what he said.

"What?" she asked.

"I said, I think I have an idea for your mask."

"Oh."

"I think if you had a little more glycerin, you'll get the consistency you're looking for."

He stepped next to her and grabbed a clean beaker and began mixing things together.

"That should do it."

Giselle took the beaker and looked at the concoction he'd put together.

"It looks so much better. Thank you."

"And thank you," Ian replied.

"Don't thank me quite yet," she said. "We have to see if the bath bomb sticks together once they're dry."

"We can check it in the morning. I think it's time to call it a night."

"I agree."

They cleaned up their work areas and hung their coats up outside of the lab.

"Do you work late hours like this at your restaurant?" Giselle asked as they headed toward the elevator.

"Yeah, oftentimes later than this because of clean up."

"I guess it's different from being on a cooking contest show."

"You watched that?" Ian asked, with a reticent smile.

"Of course I did," she said. "All of Sweet Rapids did. Your parents had a viewing party when you made it to the finals. And when you won, your parents wouldn't stop talking about it for weeks."

"Yeah, I didn't know about that until after my dad died," Ian revealed.

"Really?"

The elevator doors slid open and they got on.

Ian nodded and shoved his hands into the front pockets of his jeans.

"Dad wasn't pleased when none of us hopped right on the family business train. He griped about it so often."

"You may not have been working here, but that doesn't mean he wasn't proud."

"I know that," Ian said. "At least he made sure to tell us before...it was one of the last things he told us."

Giselle felt a lump rise in her throat. She could tell that it was still hard for him to talk about his late father.

They rode the rest of the way down the elevator in silence; until her stomach growled. She covered her face, embarrassed.

"Hungry?" Ian asked, his lip quirking upward.

"I'm starving." Giselle said, looking up at him with a wry grin.

"I noticed you skipped lunch today."

"Yeah, I was finishing up on some formulas for a few beauty products. I wanted to get them started in mass production for the test groups next week." And she also wasn't in the mood to have lunch with Thomas again.

"You've got to take care of yourself."

Giselle laughed. "You sound like my sister."

The elevator dinged and they walked off. Once they were in the parking lot, Ian escorted her to her car.

"Hey," she started before she lost her nerve. "You wanna go and pick something up to eat?"

Ian seemed to hesitate, and then said, "I'm actually late for dinner with my Mom."

"Oh! I'm sorry. Don't let me keep you."

"Do you want to join us?"

She was surprised by his offer.

"Oh...thanks, but I couldn't possibly–"

"She won't mind."

Giselle smiled but politely declined.

"Maybe we can raincheck, then?" he asked. "I'll cook."

She shouldn't agree. She shouldn't have even asked him if he wanted to go out for food in the first place.

Despite all of that, she found herself saying, "That would be great."

Giselle was in the supply closet late one night, when she heard the door open. Ian walked in and smiled at her.

"Hey."

"Hey," she replied, and then rushed toward him, eyes wide. The heavy can of argan oil she'd been using to keep the door propped open shifted. "Ian! Don't let the door close! It's..."

Ian turned quickly but wasn't quick enough.

"Broken."

"What?" he asked. "Broken?"

He reached for the doorknob and jiggled it.

"Stand back," he said.

"What are you going to do, Ian?" Giselle asked.

"I'm going to try and force it open."

Giselle chuckled and took a step back. Ian was obviously strong, from the muscles that bulged beneath his shirt, but she didn't think that even he was a match against the steel door. Ian slammed his shoulder against the door, but it didn't budge. After a few tries, he banged on the door.

"Ian, everyone else is gone." She looked at her phone. "The night guard won't be through for a few hours."

Ian sighed and turned to face her, his back pressed against the door.

"I'm sorry about getting us stuck in here."

"I've been in worse predicaments," she murmured as she scrolled through her phone. Maybe she could call Thomas. "Damn, no signal."

"I guess your boyfriend won't be coming to save the day then."

Giselle looked up at Ian, confused. "Boyfriend?"

Ian gave her a knowing look and she rolled her eyes, agitated. "I already told you. There's nothing going on between Thomas and me."

"Does *he* know that?" Ian asked, propping one foot against the door and crossing his arms across his chest.

"Of course he knows that."

"You keep going out with him nearly every day, you may be sending him mixed signals."

"It's just lunch. And we're co-workers. I go out with other co-workers for lunch all of the time."

"You haven't gone out with me for lunch."

"You haven't asked," Giselle said.

"And you haven't offered," Ian replied.

Giselle sighed. "Why do you care so much? Are you jealous or something?"

"Of *Walsh*?" Ian laughed. "Not in this lifetime. Or the next."

"Why are you so concerned about how I spend my time with him then?"

Ian pushed off of the door and walked toward her.

"Because Thomas Walsh is a no good son of a bitch and if you can't see that, then maybe you aren't as smart as everyone says you are."

"Fuck you, Ian."

He was in her face now and getting on her nerves.

And turning her on at the same time.

His mouth spread into a wolfish grin. "Are you finally offering?"

"'Finally offering'?" she repeated.

The nerve of his arrogant ass. So what if it was true that she desired Ian in a way that she'd never desired any other man before?

She stood there, glaring at him as her body grew more and more aroused every second that passed with him watching her like he could read her mind.

She wanted to smack that grin off of his face.

But instead, she found herself letting out a growl as she lunged at him. And crushed her lips to his.

Chapter Ten

The last vestige of Ian's self-control snapped when he felt Giselle's full, lush lips on his. The momentum of her throwing her body against his had him stumbling backward and his back hit the door.

He pressed his tongue against the seam of her lips and she didn't hesitate to open her mouth for him. The moment their tongues touched, the sensation of desire that had been simmering amplified.

His eyes flew open when he heard her gasp and felt her hands against his chest pushing him away. She ended the kiss as abruptly as she'd initiated it.

"Oh, God," she said, covering her lips. "I'm sorry."

"It's okay, Giselle," he said, slightly out of breath.

"No," she said, shaking her head and squeezing her eyes shut. She turned away from him and walked away. It only took a few steps to reach the other side of the closet. "I said I wouldn't do this."

"Do...what?" he asked, although he was pretty sure he knew. He'd told himself the exact same thing numerous times.

"You."

"You said you wouldn't do...me?" he asked, trying to hide the amused grin on his face.

"Yes...No!" She blew out a frustrated breath and ran her fingers through her hair. The style was different now. The braids were gone and now her hair was a deep burgundy. It was still pulled up into a bun, showing off the tapered fade on the sides and back of her head. He wondered what her hair looked like down. He knew she wore it up to avoid any hazards at work. But, more times than he wanted to admit, he wanted to know what it felt like to pull out that bun and run his fingers through her hair.

"I said I wouldn't get involved with you," she said, breaking his thoughts. "Like...this."

Ian decided the best course of action was to be completely honest with her.

"I told myself the same thing."

She looked up at him when he finally spoke.

"You did?"

"Yes. But Giselle, we've danced around this for over a month now. And I'm more attracted to you now than ever."

Which was out of the ordinary for him. He'd tried to chalk it up to the fact that he hadn't been with a woman since before he'd left Vegas and returned home; but he knew better. Something about Giselle Warren called out to a part of Ian that he'd always thought was unreachable.

"This is a bad idea."

"Why?" he asked.

"I just get the feeling that getting involved with you is going to bring nothing but trouble."

He reached out to her, wrapping one hand around her waist to pull her against his body. The other hand palmed her cheek in a caress as he leaned down, touching his nose to hers.

"Something tells me trouble is your middle name."

"It's actually Tania," she whispered, smiling.

"Giselle Tania."

Her chest was rising and falling rapidly, as his lips hovered just above hers.

"I want you, Giselle. And I know you want me too. Aren't you tired of fighting it? I sure as hell am."

He watched her as she visibly swallowed, and then licked her lips.

"I am tired of fighting it," she finally admitted.

"Good," he said, before closing his mouth over hers again.

In the next instant they were shoving each other's lab coats off.

He swiftly walked her backwards, until her back hit the opposite wall, and then hoisted her up into his arms. The movement caused her skirt to ride up to her waist, revealing a sexy pair of black lace panties. Her arousal filled his nostrils and his erection throbbed even harder.

He broke the kiss from her lips and traced the shell of her ear with the tip of his tongue before pulling her earlobe between his lips. When he reached her neck, he grazed his teeth against the delicate skin, and her hips jerked against his stomach. He grabbed her panties with both hands and tore the flimsy fabric off.

Her eyes grew wide as she looked down.

"Those were from Scarlette's Closet!" she scowled, referring to the high end lingerie boutique that had recently open in Reno.

"Sweetheart, I don't give a damn what they were," he said, wrapping an arm around her waist. "All I know is they were in the way of what I really want right now."

"Ian, do you know how much those cost–"

He shut her up by kissing her again, letting his tongue dive deeply into her mouth, as his fingers plunged inside of her at the same time.

"I'll buy you a new pair," he offered, when he finally came

up for air. He continued pumping his fingers in and out of her and her head fell back against the wall. She let out a sexy moan and began to move against his hand. Her skin grew flush and her moans filled the small room. When he felt her clench around his fingers, he pulled away.

He needed to be inside of her.

She opened her eyes and looked at him with a sexy grin. Her eyes were now half closed but full of lust. She reached down between them and undid his jeans. She kept her eyes locked with his as she reached into his briefs and wrapped her hand around his dick. As soon as she began to stroke him, his eyes drifted closed and he tightened his grip on her waist.

"Fuck, Giselle," he growled.

"I thought that's what we were doing," she teased, with a seductive purr in his ear.

"Oh...we're about to."

He reached in his back pocket for his wallet and quickly grabbed a condom. He shoved his jeans further down, ripped open the condom and sheathed himself. Then he cupped her ass with both hands as she propped her legs up on the supply shelves that flanked them, causing her to be wide open for him.

She looked so good like that, ready and waiting for him. He couldn't wait a minute longer. He slammed into her and the force caused the shelves to rattle on either side of Ian and Giselle. If the damn things hadn't been screwed into the wall, they would have knocked them over for sure. He pulled out slowly, before driving into her again.

Giselle's nails dug into his shoulders and he continued; languidly pulling out before diving inside of her again.

Their scent filled the closet and it turned him on even more. He sped up his pace as he gripped her cheeks tighter.

"Ian," she whimpered. "I'm going to–"

"Do it," he rasped. "Come for me, sweetheart."

And she did, her head fell back against the wall again, as

she screamed. Her own thrusts became wild and out of control. His body tightened and he wrapped his hand around her neck and kissed her as he felt his release.

He continued kissing her slowly as they both rode the last waves of their orgasms.

Ian pulled out of Giselle and eased her to her feet, her dress falling back in to place; though it was now wrinkled. She looked down and saw her ridiculously expensive panties in shreds on the floor. Ian turned away as he removed the condom and fixed his clothes.

The room was filled with silence until he turned back around to face her.

"Giselle–" he said, quietly.

Shit, he regrets it already.

"I understand," she said, quickly.

"You understand what?" he asked, perplexed.

"That this...it was just sex. I know you're not someone who is in to commitments. And to be honest, neither am I. So...we're good."

"Actually," Ian said, clearing his throat. "I was going to ask if you'd..."

"If I'd what?"

"Go out with me tomorrow night."

Giselle's mouth fell open and she could feel her cheeks darken.

Ian's lip tilted upward. "You turn purple when you blush."

"I..."

"So, what do you say, Giselle. Will you go out with me tomorrow night?"

"I...um...yes," she said, nodding. "Yes. I'll go out with you tomorrow night."

Ian nodded and gave her another smile. She could tell this was something new for him. But if he was willing to take a shot, then she was too.

He reached out and pushed a curly strand of hair out of her face. It had fallen out of its bun when he had her up against the wall.

"I hadn't gotten the chance to tell you yet, but I like the new hairstyle."

"Thanks. I change it a lot."

"That doesn't surprise me one bit."

Ian Noble was surprising her though.

"Miss Warren? Are you in here?"

Giselle let out a sigh of relief. She rushed to the door.

"Albert! Yes, we got stuck in here," she called out to the night guard.

"I'll have you out in just a minute."

They heard the turning of a key and a moment later the door opened.

"Thank you so much," she said. "I was afraid that we would have been stuck in there all night."

If they could keep doing what they'd just finished doing, it might not have been so bad.

"I did my walk through early and saw that you hadn't cleaned up and left yet. Then I saw this can here," Albert said, kicking the makeshift door prop.

"We're so glad you did," Giselle said.

His eyes grew wide when he saw Ian standing behind her. "Evening, Mr. Noble."

"Good evening, Albert," Ian said. Giselle could hear the smile in his voice. "Thank you again for getting us out of there."

"Not a problem, sir. Not a problem at all," he tipped his security guard hat. "I've got to finish making my rounds and get back down to the first floor."

"Don't let us keep you."

After Albert walked off, Ian went back into the supply closet and picked up their lab coats. He handed Giselle hers and they headed back to the lab. She also noticed that he'd picked up her torn panties and shoved them into his back pocket.

"I think I'm done working for tonight," Giselle said.

Ian nodded. "Yeah, me too."

They put their things away and left. By the time they reached the first floor, Albert was back at the security desk. They waved good-bye and thanked him again for getting them out of the supply closet.

"What time should I pick you up tomorrow?"

"What?" Giselle asked. She'd been lost in her own thoughts, replaying what had happened between them.

"Dinner?" Ian reminded her as they stopped at her car. "What time should I pick you up?"

"Seven?"

"Okay. Can I get your phone number, so I can call or text you when I'm on my way?"

"Yeah, give me your phone."

He reached into his pocket, pulled out his phone and handed it to her. She plugged her name and number in his phone.

"Here. Shoot me a text with your name so I'll know it's you, and I'll send you my address."

He took the phone back and she hit the unlock button on her key fob.

"I'll see you tomorrow," Giselle said.

Ian didn't speak again. Instead, he leaned down and kissed her lips. This one was different from the other kisses. It was unhurried and gentle. It was sweet.

"Get home safely."

Giselle nodded, opened her car door and got in.

Once she got home, she shut the door and leaned against it.

What the hell had she done?

She'd had sex.

With Ian Noble.

In a supply closet!

And it was amazing, she thought as a smile curved her lips.

She moved through her apartment to her bedroom, to the en suite bathroom and turned on the shower. His scent was all over her.

She took a long shower, replaying the night's events in her head over and over. When she finally got out of the shower, she noticed she had a text message on her phone.

Unknown number: Hey, this is Ian. Save my number.

Done. My address is 4021 Harter Street, Apt. 307

Ian: Did you make it home okay?

Giselle smiled at his concern and typed out a reply.

Yes, I just got out of the shower actually.

Ian: Damn, maybe I should have followed you home.

Giselle laughed out loud at his response.

Good night Ian.

Ian: Hey, Giselle...

What?

It took him so long, Giselle thought maybe he wasn't going to respond back. Finally her phone pinged again and she looked down at the message.

Ian: It wasn't just sex.

Chapter Eleven

The bell rang over Everetts' Bakery as Ian walked in Saturday afternoon.

Tessa and Dana looked up and smiled as he made his way to the countertop.

"Hello ladies," he said, speaking to the sisters.

"Hey, Ian!" Dana said. A bell rang out from the kitchen and Dana turned. "That's the next batch of cupcakes. I'll go and get them."

Tessa came from behind the counter and gave Ian a sisterly hug.

"How are you, Ian?"

"I'm good."

Tessa nodded before heading behind the counter again. "Are you getting some bear claws for Miss Irene?"

He moved closer to the counter. "Actually..." He rubbed the back of his neck. He couldn't believe this shit. He actually felt...nervous. "Do you know Giselle Warren?"

Tessa's eyes lit up. "Of course I know Giselle." She gave him a teasing grin as she said, "Isaiah told me about your first meeting."

Ian grinned as well. "Yeah, we've since called a truce. Everything has been smooth sailing since then."

"So I've heard."

Ian's eyebrows narrowed. "What exactly has my brother been telling you?"

Tessa placed her hand over her chest, her face a mask of innocence. "Nothing!" she said, as she moved over to the display case and opened it. She grabbed several cupcakes and placed them in a box.

Ian continued to stare at her unconvinced. She looked at him again as she closed the box.

"Okay," she relented. "He may have mentioned to me when he came by to have lunch with me earlier that the night guard might have told Isaiah about finding you and Giselle trapped in the closet last night."

Ian bit back a groan.

"Was that all he said?"

"Yep."

The last thing he needed were rumors going around that someone had heard what had gone on between the two of them the night before.

It was spontaneous and hot and downright amazing.

And he couldn't wait to have her again.

But first...the date.

For the first time since probably ever, Ian desired to be with a woman for more than one night. He thought about Giselle nonstop. And despite the previous night's events, he didn't just want her in his bed. She was smart, funny and witty; and Ian wanted to know what made Giselle tick. During the day, when he wasn't thinking of work, he was thinking of her. And at nights, she invaded his dreams.

"Hello...Earth to Ian."

Ian blinked and looked at Tessa who was staring at him, waving her hand in front of his face.

"Sorry," he said. "Guess I zoned out."

"Something on your mind? Or someone?"

Tessa pushed the box of cupcakes toward him.

"What are these?" he asked.

"Tiramisu cupcakes," she said. Then she leaned forward and whispered, "They're Giselle's favorite."

Ian smiled and reached for his wallet, but Tessa waved him off. "This batch is on the house."

Ian picked up the box and gave Tessa a quick kiss on the cheek. "Thanks, Tessa."

Isaiah better hurry the hell up and propose to that woman, Ian thought as he walked out of the bakery.

Ten minutes before seven, Giselle's doorbell rang.

She blew out a breath, ran her fingers through her hair that she'd blown out and flat ironed and headed for the door.

She opened it and smiled when she saw Ian standing in the doorway, holding a pastry box. He also had a familiar bag hooked on his finger.

"You didn't!" she said as he held the bag out to her.

"I told you I'd buy you a new pair," Ian said, as Giselle looked in the Scarlette's Closet bag.

He stepped into her apartment and pulled her into his arms before he leaned down and kissed her.

"Are you ready to go?" he asked.

"Yeah, let me just put this away."

She was just about to turn and head to her bedroom when she noticed a strange look on Ian's face. She turned to see what he was looking at and saw her silks hanging from the ceiling.

He walked over to it, then around it.

Finally, he turned back and looked at her. He tilted his

head to the side, his eyes studying her body from head to toe. Then his eyes grew wide.

"You're Gypsy," he realized, pointing a finger at her.

"Frank did say you were a fan," Giselle said, with a smirk.

"Wait a minute," he said, walking back over to her. "You *knew* I'd been coming to your shows."

"Yes," she admitted.

"Why didn't you say anything?" he asked.

She ran her hand up his chest as her eyes drifted down to his lap. "I liked watching you squirm."

She moved around him and headed to the bedroom to put the bag he'd brought her on the dresser, and then returned to him.

He was shaking his head with a grin on his face.

"What's so funny?" she asked.

"That first day we met..."

"When we nearly tore each other's heads off, you mean?"

"Yes," he said, still smiling. "When I turned around and first saw you, I swear it felt like we'd met before. But I wasn't going to dare ask you if we had, because I knew it would sound like bullshit."

She smiled and pointed at the box. "Is that from Everetts'?"

"Yes."

"What's in there?" she asked, moving closer to him.

Ian took a step back. "You'll find out after dinner."

They headed for the front door. Once they were outside of her apartment, Giselle locked the door and then they left the building. When they reached Ian's car, he opened the passenger door for her. Once she was strapped in, he shut the door, and hurried to the driver's side, got in, put the box in the back and started the car.

"How was your day?" he asked, as he drove down the street.

"It was fine. Worked on my new silks performance."

"For your alter ego?"

"I guess you could say that."

"I can't wait to see it."

"Maybe I can show it to you."

Ian pulled up to a stop light and looked at her.

"As in...a private show?" he asked, wiggling his eyebrows.

Giselle's head fell back against the head rest as she laughed. "You don't have to make it sound so lewd."

The light turned green and Ian pulled off. "Believe me, sweetheart, the things I did to you in those silks in my dreams were very lewd."

"We may have to try some of them out one day."

She noticed his grip on the steering wheel tighten.

"I swear if we didn't have reservations, I'd turn this car around right now."

"And where exactly do we have reservations?"

"You'll see when we get there," he said.

They joked and talked as they drove north into Carson City. They pulled up to a popular restaurant.

When they entered the restaurant, Giselle looked around, confused.

"I thought you said we had reservations."

"We do," he said, as he took her hand and led her through the dining area and to the back.

"But...no one's here."

"I know."

They went into the kitchen, and he led her over to a pair of stools that were at the work island. Ian pulled one out for Giselle, and after she sat down, he slid the stool forward, before leaning over her shoulder to kiss her neck.

Giselle looked around the kitchen.

"Are you...are you going to cook for me?"

Ian winked at her, and then grabbed an apron.

"I'm cashing in on that rain check."

Chapter Twelve

Ian stirred the beurre blanc sauce he'd just finished one last time.

"Giselle," he said. "Come here."

He heard the stool scrape against the floor as she pushed it back and then walked over to him. He picked up a clean spoon, dipped it into the sauce and held it up. He blew it slightly then pushed the spoon toward her lips.

"Taste."

Giselle smiled as she opened her mouth and wrapped her lips around the spoon.

"Mmm," she moaned. "That is decadent."

Ian leaned forward and kissed her lips. "First course will be ready soon."

"This is just the first course?" Giselle asked as she went back to her seat and picked up the wine he'd poured for her before he started cooking.

"Of course it is."

He seasoned the scallops that he had pulled out of the industrial fridge and dredged them in a bit of flour before putting them in the hot skillet. He seared them on each side for a couple of minutes and then he placed them on their plates. He went back to the fridge and got the sauce he'd made and drizzled it around and on top of the scallops. He garnished it with some chopped chives and then carried the plates over to the island.

"Are you ready for a seafood extravaganza that will have you melting in your seat?" he asked, sitting the plate down in front of her with a flourish.

"This looks amazing."

He'd never cared about impressing a woman with his cooking before. But tonight, Ian sat on the edge of his seat, waiting as Giselle cut into the scallop covered in beurre blanc sauce. She bit into the food and her body sank further into the seat, as a look of rapture covered her face.

"Good?" he asked, with a satisfied smile, before he began eating off of his own plate.

"Good?" Giselle shook her head. "Ian this is amazing. I can't wait to see what the next course is."

They quickly finished and Ian took their plates and put them in the sink.

"So what's next?" Giselle asked.

"Brown butter risotto with lobster," Ian said.

"Sounds heavenly."

He'd put the lobster tails in a pot to boil before he sat down to eat with Giselle, and now they were ready. He drained the water and set the lobsters off to the side to cool off. He then put a pot of chicken stock on to boil, and he turned back to the island and began quickly chopping an onion.

"It always amazes me how cooks can chop so fast like that," Giselle said.

"It's actually not that hard."

"Yeah, right," she scoffed.

"I'm serious," Ian said. "Come here, I'll show you."

Giselle went to the sink, washed her hand and after she

dried them on a clean towel, went and stood next to Ian. He pulled her in front him and wrapped his arms around her body.

"First of all, a good quality knife is key."

"Of course a chef would say that," Giselle teased.

Ian playfully swatted her on her backside. "Pay attention. The date will be ruined if you chop off of a finger."

"Yes, chef," Giselle crooned. The sexy way she'd just said that had his dick stirring to life. This woman was something else.

"Pick up the knife," he ordered.

When she had it in her hand, he moved her fingers around. "Hold it like this...that's right."

He wrapped his hand around her wrist. "This is the motion in which you chop." He guided her wrist a few times and when he felt her doing it well on her own he let go.

He then took her other hand. "You'll keep your fingers curved...like this. So they stay out of the way of the knife. Your knuckles will rest against the flat part the knife. Make sure they stay parallel."

He guided her again, this time his hands on both wrists. When she seemed to have the hang of it, he placed the onion in front of her.

"Give it a shot," he said.

He watched her movements over her shoulder as she quickly chopped the onions.

"Perfect," he said.

She sat the knife down and turned around in his arm. He was startled for a moment when he saw tears in her eyes.

"Now what is the trick to keep from crying while chopping and onion?"

He pulled the small handkerchief out of his vest pocket and dabbed the moisture from her cheek.

"Breath through your mouth, not your nose."

"I'll keep that in mind."

She went back to her seat and he started working on the risotto.

"I have to redeem myself since you caused me to screw this dish up the last time I made it."

"Me?" Giselle asked, confused. "How did I cause you to screw it up when this is the first time you've cooked for me?"

"I was cooking it for myself one night at home and was distracted."

"I see," she said, quietly.

He didn't know why he'd admitted that to her. But he felt like he could be completely open and honest around her.

"Since we're being honest," Giselle said, in a tone that made him look over his shoulder at her as he stirred the rice. "You were a distraction to me even before we met."

"I was?"

Giselle nodded.

"I saw the video of your fight in Vegas."

Ian rolled his eyes and turned back to face the stove.

"Of course you did."

"Thomas showed it to me at lunch one day."

"Of course he did," Ian scoffed.

"Okay," Giselle said. "What is the deal between you two? Obviously, you have some kind of history."

Ian turned away from the stove and sat the wooden spoon down before looking up at her.

"When we were teenagers, there was this girl–"

"Of course, it was over a girl," Giselle teased.

"Anyway," Ian continued. "She liked me, but apparently Walsh had it in his mind that she was his already. Sound familiar?"

Giselle ignored his smart remark and asked, "So what happened?"

"He called himself trying to confront me on it. He tried to get physical."

"What did you do?" Giselle gasped, slightly shocked. Walsh had probably never seemed like the confrontational type to her, until Ian had shown up.

"I broke the bastard's nose."

"I see."

"Look, now that that's out in the open, can we not discuss Walsh anymore? I really can't stand that guy."

"Of course."

He turned to check on the risotto. "So what did you think about the video?" he asked, curiously. He wondered if her opinion of him was any different now.

"I was strangely...turned on by it."

He looked over his shoulder again. He hadn't expected *that* for an answer.

"You were?"

"It was obvious you were defending yourself. That guy hauled off and hit you first."

"Yeah," Ian sighed. "But with good cause, I suppose."

"What's the story behind *that*?"

He paused from stirring the risotto and hesitated.

"No judgement here," she said, in a tone that had him wanting to tell her his entire life story.

"It seems that I, *unknowingly...*" He made sure to put emphasis on that. "Slept with his wife."

"Whoa," she said.

He shook his head. "Yeah."

"Still not judging, but...how?"

"A lot of women come to Vegas looking for a spontaneous hook up."

"And you were willing to oblige."

"I was before..."

"Before what?"

He turned when he realized she was standing directly behind him. He studied her. What was different about *her*? He'd been with more women than he could count. Lots of them were beautiful, or smart, or funny, or great in bed.

But Giselle was all of that and more.

"Before you," he finally said, quietly.

"Before me?" she asked. "Why me?"

"That's just it!" he said, animatedly. "I have *no* idea. I don't understand what the fuck is going on between us. I've never experienced anything like this before."

Giselle looked down, but Ian grabbed her chin and lifted it so her eyes would meet his.

"But I do know one thing. I'm willing to explore it, see where it goes, if you are."

Giselle nodded and smiled. "I'm definitely willing."

He pulled her closer to him before wrapping his arms around her waist and lowering his mouth to hers.

Her arms slid around his neck as his tongue tangled with hers. Her own sweet flavor mixed with the savoriness of the meal.

"Ian," she moaned against his lips.

"Hmm?" he said, still kissing her.

"You're going to burn your risotto again."

He chuckled and pressed his forehead to hers for a minute and then turned back to the stove.

He wasn't about to ruin his best dish again.

Chapter Thirteen

"So, how'd you like the risotto?"

Giselle looked over at Ian as he handed her a dish to rinse off. They were standing side by side washing the dishes. Ian insisted that she didn't have to help, but Giselle wouldn't hear of it.

"I see why you won that cooking show," she said. "That was the best damn risotto I've ever tasted."

She noticed his smile as he nodded. "I'm glad you enjoyed it."

"Don't be surprised if I ask you to make it for me again."

"Any time you want it, consider it done."

For some reason, him saying that warmed her inside.

"Come on," he said, after they finished washing the dishes. "Let's go to the dining area and have the dessert."

"I've been dying to know what you brought from Everetts'."

"I could tell by the way you kept eyeing the box."

Giselle led the way out of the kitchen and Ian turned the light off behind them. Once they were sitting at a table, he opened the box and her nose took in the familiar scent.

"These are my absolute favorite cupcakes from Everetts',"

she said, reaching into the box. She swiped a large dollop of icing onto her finger and stuck it in her mouth.

Her eyes drifted close as she moaned. When she opened her eyes, Ian was staring intently at her.

"What?" she asked, her pulse spiking at his salacious gaze.

"You have no idea how fucking sexy that sound is. Especially when I'm the reason you're making it."

She hid her face as she took a small bite from the cupcake. After she finished it, she looked up again and asked, "What was it like being on TV?"

He grinned at her before answering. He knew she was changing the subject. He leaned back, stretched his legs out in front of him and draped his arm over the back of the chair.

"I loved it. It was a lot of fun, even though it was a lot of pressure to impress the judges."

"Well you did a great job, obviously. The town went nuts when you made it to the finals. You should have seen..."

She stopped, instantly regretting not thinking before she spoke.

"It's okay," Ian said. "You can talk about him."

She gave him a soft smile. "Your father was *so* proud; of all four of you."

Ian let out a sigh. He remembered her saying that before. "That was something I used to wish I heard a lot more of. But he did make sure to let us know that he was proud, before he..." He paused and visibly swallowed. "It was one of the last things he told us."

"That's a good thing."

"Yeah. We always assumed he was completely against our decisions to pursue other goals beyond Noble Naturals, but after he died, Isaiah told me he was cleaning out Dad's office and found a box full of stuff."

"What kind of stuff?" Giselle asked.

"Articles, videos, pictures...you name it; any way we were publicly acknowledged, he kept some kind of memorabilia."

"Wow."

"Yeah."

They sat in silence for a few contemplative moments before Ian blew out a breath and sat up.

"So, how did you end up working for my family's company?"

Now he was the one changing the subject. He didn't want to talk about his dad anymore, and she understood why.

"Oh, I've dreamt of working at Noble Naturals forever."

"Really?" Ian asked, surprised.

Giselle nodded. "My mother used the products on our hair when I was a girl. She raved about how great they were. And I loved mixing and creating my own hair products, lotions and even makeup. So it just seemed like the perfect match, me working there, helping to create things. When Isaiah came in last year with the idea of expanding the company with new and different kinds of beauty products, I was so excited."

"Yeah, that was a pretty great idea on his part," Ian said. "Isaiah said you've been here for years?"

"I got an internship right out of college and worked my way up. I was determined, so I went to school out here, rather than staying close to home. Needless to say, my family had a hard time with me moving across the country."

"Where is home?" he asked.

"North Carolina."

"I thought I heard a bit of a southern accent."

"People teased me about that all of the time when I first got here."

"I think it's sexy," he said. She smiled at his comment and took another bite of her cupcake.

"What's your family like?" he asked.

She smiled warmly, thinking of them. "My parents are great."

"I remember you saying you had a sister. Do you have any more siblings?"

"No, it's just me and Ciara."

"Are you close?"

"Like you wouldn't believe."

Ian chuckled. "I shared a womb and a large portion of my life with three siblings. I might be able to imagine a little."

"What was *that* like?" she asked.

Ian thought about it for a moment before saying, "It was the absolute best and worst thing in the world."

Giselle laughed at his response.

"It's true," Ian said laughing with her. "On one hand, you know that they will always be there for you. On the other hand, they were *always* there."

"They've always got your back, even though they may drive you completely insane," Giselle said.

"That's it right there."

She was on her second cupcake by now. She pushed the box away. "Okay, you have to take these, otherwise I'll eat them all. And my ass doesn't need that."

"Your ass is perfect," he said.

She was suddenly filled with the memory of the night before and the way his large hands had a firm grip on her butt as he took her against the wall in the supply closet.

Ian looked at his watch. "Our time is almost up here."

"Okay...I have to ask?" Giselle said. The question had been running through her mind from the moment they walked into the empty restaurant.

"Ask what?" Ian said, closing the box of desserts.

"How did you pull this off? Getting this entire restaurant for the two of us?"

"Oh, Wally and I go way back."

"*Wally*?" she said, referring to Walter Lowe, the owner of the restaurant. She'd never heard him referred to by that name.

"Yeah."

To him, it didn't seem like a big deal. But to Giselle, it was, by far, the best first date she'd ever gone on.

"Well, please tell 'Wally' I said thanks for this."

"I'll make sure he gets the message," Ian said as they left the restaurant and headed to the car.

Giselle was quiet on the ride back to her apartment.

Shockingly, she felt nervous about what would happen when they reached her door. She typically had no qualms about inviting a man in and was very clear about what she wanted from said man.

But *this* man.

Nothing about what she felt for Ian Noble made sense from the very beginning, she thought as they rode the elevator up to her floor. Considering they'd already gone at it like two horny teenagers the night before, she should have been able to just yank him into her apartment and have her way with him.

Instead, her fingers trembled as she pulled her keys out of her purse. She looked down at her shoes, her hair falling into her face.

"Do you..." The timid sound of her voice, made her shake her head.

This is not you, she chastised herself. *You are Giselle Warren goddammit, not some shy girl. Lift up your fucking head.*

She steeled her spine, lifted her head high and damn near melted at the sight of his gorgeous eyes looking down at her.

"Do you want to come in?"

His hands were in his pants pockets as if he were fighting to keep from touching her.

"Any other night, I'd say hell yes," Ian said. "But I've got a brunch date with Irene Noble in the morning."

"Oh," she said, feel slightly deflated. "I can't say I'm not disappointed a little. But I understand."

"I guess I'll have to catch that private show another night," he said, referring to her silks.

"What makes you think I was going to give you a show tonight?"

He finally removed his hands from his pockets and reached out to her, wrapping one arm around her waist to pull her flush against him, while the other hand ran through the layered strands of her silky hair, before cupping the back of her neck.

"I would have asked incredibly nicely," he said as his lips lowered to hers.

Her body shivered at the connection and her mouth open immediately when she felt his tongue. He groaned as he kissed her as if he didn't want to stop. She didn't want him to stop, especially when she felt his erection against her belly.

Deciding to show him a little of what he'd be missing out on tonight, she ground her hips against him and felt him grow even harder. He groaned again and swore under his breath; and then she felt him release his hold from the back of her head.

Her body heated as his fingers dug into her thigh. He rocked against her, mimicking what he clearly wanted to be doing to her. Memories of the night before and the way he'd taken her flooded her memory and made her body cream with desire.

"You smell so sweet," he rasped in her ear. He lifted her leg and hooked it around his waist as his hand crept beneath her dress.

Anyone of her neighbors could walk out and catch them, but she couldn't care less. Especially when he slid her panties to the side and hooked two fingers inside of her.

She let out a moan as he slowly pumped his fingers in and out of her.

"Ian," she whimpered.

"Ssshh," he whispered against her lips, before speeding up the movement of his hand between her thighs. Every inch of her body coiled, before snapping. She felt her walls clamping around his fingers as she slowly came down from the high he'd taken her on.

He removed his hand from inside of her and she trembled again as she watched him bring his fingers to his mouth.

"I can't wait to *really* taste you," he said, never taking his eyes off of hers.

Her eyes drifted down to his pants again.

"Are you sure you don't want to come in?"

"No," he admitted. "But I know if I come in, I'm going to want to stay all night."

"Right," she said, remembering what he'd said earlier. "Brunch with your mother."

"Yeah," Ian said, clearly regretting his plans, even though they were with his mother.

"Like I said, I understand. I think it's sweet how close you are with your mother."

"Well, after not coming home much over the last year, it's the least I can do."

Giselle figured Ian hadn't come home because it was hard to visit Sweet Rapids and not see his father.

"Yes, you don't want to piss Miss Irene off."

"No," Ian chuckled. "Definitely don't want to do that."

She watched as he shoved his hands into his pockets again. If she had pockets, she'd do the same. So she settled for clasping her hands together behind her back.

She turned and finally unlocked and opened her apartment door.

"I had a great time tonight," she said. "I'm glad I got to finally get to taste the cooking of the nationally acclaimed Chef Ian Noble."

He shook his head modestly. "Whatever, Giselle."

"Don't act coy now," she teased. She was intrigued by this side of him. He rightfully earned those accolades and she was sure he'd used them to his advantage in the past. He had that arrogant air about him. But right now, he didn't seem to want to bask in the praise.

"Go into your apartment, before I end up fucking you against the wall again."

She smiled at him. It wasn't a threat in the least. It was a promise that she'd love for him to make good on. But she decided to behave...for now.

"Have a good night, Ian," she said, stepping into her place.

"I don't know how good it will be," he said. For some reason, the fact that he was showing so much restraint made her want him even more. "I'll see you at work on Monday. Lock the door."

She nodded, shut the door and locked it.

And then she went to her bedroom, opened the nightstand drawer and pulled out one of her little battery powered friends.

Chapter Fourteen

"Ian...Ian?"

Ian blinked and looked up at his mother and smiled.

"Sorry, Mom. What did you say?"

"Where is your head at this morning?" she asked.

Not where he wanted it to be, which was between Giselle's legs tasting her sweetness. He shook his head to try and clear those thoughts from his mind.

Irene set her Mimosa down and studied her son.

"You look dreadful, sweetheart."

Ian smiled and took a sip of his drink. Irene Noble was never one to hold her tongue.

"I didn't get a lot of sleep last night."

"Being out late will do that."

Ian chuckled. "I wasn't out late, actually. I made sure to try and get some rest before my date with one of my best girls."

"Oh, boy," Irene said, waving her hand at him. "Save that Noble charm for some other woman...like Giselle."

Ian coughed on his drink. He hit his chest with his fist a few times before looking up at his mother.

"Giselle? Warren?"

"That's the only Giselle I know," Irene said, as she daintily unfolded her cloth napkin and placed it across her lap. She looked up at him with a smirk and a knowing look in her eye. "I'm old but I'm not blind, son. I've seen the way the two of you work together."

"Giselle is an extremely intelligent woman. And her ideas are gr–"

"I also see the way you look at her."

First his brother, now his mother seemed to take notice of the way he obviously couldn't keep his eyes off of Giselle.

"What's going on between the two of you?" Irene asked.

Ian shrugged as he dug into his food. No sense in bullshitting with his mother. She'd see right through it. "We went out last night."

And all night he'd regretted not going into her apartment. He was tired this morning anyway; at least it would have been worth it if he'd been able to be with Giselle, rather than mere the thoughts of her and his hand.

Irene perked up at those words.

"And?"

"And...nothing, Mom." *Unfortunately*.

"Oh come on!" Irene said. "How was the date?"

Ian set his fork down and looked at his mother. "It was nice."

Irene nodded, seeming content with that answer. "Good. I like Giselle. She's...full of life. Like you."

For some reason that made him think of the conversation he and Irene had a couple of months ago.

"Hey Mom..."

Why was he about to ask her this?

"Yes, baby?"

"Do you remember the conversation we had when I first got back home?"

"Refresh my memory," she said with a grin.

Irene knew exactly what he was talking about. She just wanted to hear him repeat it.

"About finding...'the one'," he said. "I asked you if finding your equal was what it's all about. And you said–"

"That's part of it." Irene nodded.

"What else is there?"

The curiosity was killing him. He didn't *want* to know; but he felt like he *had* to know.

Irene picked up her napkin and wiped her mouth.

"When you find that person that you absolutely can't imagine life without, when the thought of being away from them leaves an ache in your chest..." Her eyes crested with tears as she whispered, "That's how you know."

He reached over and placed his hand over hers. "I'm so sorry, Mom. I didn't mean to–"

"It's fine, Ian. Your father will always be a part of me. He's in my heart, and he's in you and your siblings. So I still get to see him every single day."

He squeezed her hand and smiled at her.

His phone rang at that moment and he pulled it out of his pocket. When he saw Michelle's name on the screen he said, "Excuse me, Mom. It's Chelle."

"Tell her I said hello," Irene said.

Ian nodded and pushed away from the table to take the call.

"What's up, Chelle?"

"Good news, Ian," Michelle said through the phone. "Looks like everything is working out and you'll be able to start back working at the restaurant in Vegas next month."

Why didn't that news excited him as much as it would have even a month ago?

"Great," he said, trying to infuse his voice with enthusiasm.

"Could you *try* to be happy about it?" Michelle said with annoyance in her voice.

"I am, Chelle. Truly. You saved my ass. Again."

"I know," she said, sighing. "Well, here's something that may make you a little more excited. The networks are still interested in giving you a show."

That did make him more excited. He thought for sure that he'd blown that opportunity out of the water.

"Really?"

"Yes. They want to set something up in a few weeks to meet. They actually want to come there to Sweet Rapids, check out your hometown."

"Just let me know when and I'll be ready."

"Good, I'll let them know. And whatever you're doing there, keep it up. Stay out of trouble."

"Yes, ma'am," he said, before hanging up.

Giselle breezed into work on Monday morning and found Ian already busy working on a body scrub they'd discussed the week before.

"Miss Warren," he said, looking up at her. His face was covered with a stylish pair of glasses and he looked delectable when he grinned at her and revealed one of those dimples she wanted to lick off of his face.

She stopped at his table, next to him, pretending to pay attention to what he was working on. "Mr. Noble."

"How was your weekend?" he asked.

"Well, it started off good," she said, planting her hand on the table.

"And it didn't end that way?"

"It just didn't end the way I would have liked."

"I'm sorry about that," he said. She heard the sincerity in his voice. "What did you do?"

She smirked and leaned toward his ear. "Myself."

She hid her grin when he dropped the bowl he'd been using. He turned and looked at her.

She watched him as he visibly swallowed and then cleared his throat.

"You...what?"

"Well, I had a little help, you know...battery powered help," she went on, chatting as if they were simply discussing the weather. "But it's not as good as the real thing."

Her eyes drifted down to his lap. She was sure his lab coat was hiding an erection. She lifted her head and locked eyes with him and noticed the look of desire in his eyes. If she wasn't careful, he just might drag her back to the supply closet. She turned on her heels and put a little extra oomph in her step as she walked over to her own lab table.

When she got there, she found him still staring at her. He finally shook his head, grinned at her and under his breath murmured, "And you say *I'm* the one who's trouble."

The door opened again and Thomas walked in as Giselle began to prepare for work. He made a beeline for her, glaring at Ian the entire time.

"Hey," he said, giving her a smile.

"Good morning," she said, returning his smile.

"We on for lunch today?"

"Oh, Thomas, I'm sorry but I already have plans."

"Really?" Thomas asked. "With who."

Giselle's eyes narrowed at Thomas. She grew annoyed by his intrusive question. "That's none of your concern."

"I just wanted to make sure you're not having lunch with..."

Her scowl deepened. Thomas was referring to Ian. "What if I am?"

"Giselle, I told you he's bad news," he said in a low voice.

"Okay," Giselle said. "We need to get something clear. Who I do or don't spend my time with is *my* business. We are co-workers, Thomas. That's. It. Is that clear?"

Thomas looked taken aback by Giselle's words. He took a step back and nodded.

"Yeah, I guess we are."

After he walked off, Giselle's eyes locked with Ian's. He raised an eyebrow and she could tell exactly what he was asking.

Are you okay?

Giselle rolled her eyes and nodded.

Ian gave a short nod, cut his eyes over to Thomas for a moment, and then went back to work.

Ian carried his lunch tray through the cafeteria. His eyes zeroed in on Giselle, who was ducked off in the back. Her face was buried in a book, as she nibbled on her sandwich.

He made his way over to her table and when she noticed him approaching, she smiled and sat her book down.

"Hey," she said.

"Do you mind if I sit with you?" he asked. "It's a bit crowded in here."

"Of course not," she said.

He sat down, grabbed the salt and pepper on the table and began working on his soup.

"How has your day been so far?" Giselle asked him as he tasted his soup, and then gave it a nod of approval.

Ian looked at her and scoffed. "It's been hard to focus on anything except the thought of you and your...'battery powered friend'."

"Oh really," Giselle said, sitting up and leaning closer to him at the table. "*How* hard?"

Ian shook his head and grinned. "Don't poke the beast, Giselle."

"Maybe I want to be poked by the beast," she needled.

Ian dropped his spoon.

"You're really asking to get fucked, aren't you?" he said, keeping his voice low, so the people around him wouldn't hear.

She giggled and went back to eating her sandwich.

"On a more serious note," Ian said. "I wanted to see if you'd go out with me again."

"I'd love to," Giselle said.

"Do you hike?" he asked.

"I haven't done it in a while," she said. "But I can definitely hold my own. I'll have to dig out my boots and dust them off."

Ian nodded. "Are you free Saturday morning?"

"Yeah. What time?"

"I'll text you to let you know, but it's probably going to be quite early."

"Okay."

They finished their lunch and headed back up to the lab.

Ian watched as she headed to her table and started back working.

He didn't know why he'd asked her to come on the trip he was about to take, but for some reason, he didn't want to do it alone.

Chapter Fifteen

"You all right, Gi?" Ian asked.

"I'm good," she said, behind him as they climbed Genoa Peak. Friday night, he'd texted her to let her know what time he would be picking her up in the morning. It was before the sunrise, but she was up and ready Saturday morning when Ian rang her doorbell.

Thankfully, he'd brought her a thermos of his specialty coffee that she was quickly becoming addicted to. He also brought some pastries they'd share once they made it to the top of the mountain.

They reached the top just as the sun began to break across the eastern horizon.

"It's beautiful up here," Giselle said, looking around. Ian stood with his back facing the sun gazing at Lake Tahoe below them. He had a peculiar look on his face. Giselle took a step forward, touching his arm.

"Ian? Are you okay?"

"My dad died a year ago today," he said in a near whisper.

"Oh, Ian," she said. He'd been quiet on the hike up, but

she just thought he was trying to focus and make sure they got up the mountain safely. "I'm so sorry."

He nodded his head, pulling his lip between his teeth. It was obvious he was attempting to keep his emotions in check. She moved her hand from his arm and hugged him around his waist.

"After the public home going ceremony we had for him, my siblings and I came up here with my mother to spread his ashes."

"Was this spot special to him?" Giselle asked.

"My mom said he proposed to her at sunrise here," he said.

Giselle imagined that it must have been beautiful.

Ian shook his head. "I must have you wanting to run back down this mountain," he said, with a sad chuckle.

"Why would you think that?"

"I didn't think how it would look, bringing you up here with me to the same spot that my father proposed to my mother."

"I'm sure you weren't thinking about that at all. You just wanted to come to the place where you said your final goodbye to your father. To be quite honest, I'm honored that you would think to bring me. But why wouldn't you do this with your brother or your mother? I'm sure they're thinking of your father and missing him a lot today as well."

"I'm meeting up with them later for lunch and we're going to video conference my sisters. I wanted to come up here before I saw them. I just needed time to myself, you know? I asked you to come with me because...I don't know. I guess I didn't exactly want to be alone and also, I feel like I can talk to you about anything. I've talked about my father to you more than anyone else since he died."

Giselle took Ian's hand and sat down on the ground, tugging him with her.

"So talk," she said, staring at him as he continued to stare out in the distance.

"It's just...it still doesn't feel real sometimes. Even though we saw his body after..." Ian shook his head, obviously trying to wipe an unpleasant memory from his brain. "Some days it's extremely difficult to grasp the idea that my father is no longer here. I regret not talking to him more or spending more time with him, just being around him."

Giselle sighed and rested her head on his shoulder.

"You can't think about him with regret. Just remember all of the good times you had together, the laughs you shared, the talks you had and the time you did have."

"Yeah," he said. After a while, he looked down at her. "Hey, thanks for coming up here with me."

"Thanks for inviting me."

They spent the rest of the early morning watching daylight cover Lake Tahoe while they ate their breakfast.

Giselle looked around at the items they would be rolling out for the first round of product testing. She was confident that they would have positive feedback.

But she was still nervous.

"Hey."

Giselle turned to find Ian walking toward her. As usual, they were the last two left in the lab.

"Don't do that," Ian said.

"Do what?" she asked, confused.

Ian stopped in front of her.

"Don't worry," he said, reaching out to brush his thumb against her temple. Her head instantly leaned into his hand, her body relaxing.

"Everything is going to be fine," he assured.

"You think so?"

"I know so. Come on, let's get out of here. I noticed you didn't eat lunch. Again."

"Yeah, I guess I forgot."

He shook his head, and took her hand in his, leading her out of the lab.

"You've got to stop doing that, Gi."

She smiled at the way he shortened her name. Most people either called her Giselle or GiGi, but only Ian called her 'Gi'. She liked it quite a bit.

After they exited the building, they went to her car.

"What are your plans for dinner?" he asked.

She hit the key fob.

"That depends on what you're cooking."

He shook his head and chuckled. "Follow me," he instructed.

She turned to open her car door, when Ian whipped her back around, pulled her to his body and kissed her.

She was breathless when he finally pulled away.

"I've been wanting to do that ever since you walked in this morning."

"I'm glad you finally did."

"Come on," he said, taking a step back. "I need to feed you."

She knew his unspoken words.

She was going to need her strength tonight.

They drove for about fifteen minutes until they reached the outskirts of town. Ian kept a close eye on Giselle's car in his rear view mirrors. There were no street lights on the private road they were on now.

His house finally came into view; solar lights lined the long paved driveway they were on and continued around the front perimeter of the house.

Ian smiled when he got out of his car and heard Giselle get out of hers as well.

"Wow."

"You like?"

He watched her face as she took in the two-story modern style home. It was steel, glass and wood; sharp, yet incredibly sleek and stylish.

They entered the house and Ian turned the lights on. Giselle turned in a full circle taking in the interior of the house, which was surrounded with floor to ceiling windows.

"You're not worried about Peeping Toms out here?" she asked with a grin.

Ian shook his head. "There isn't another house around here for a good ten miles in any direction. But I do have shades installed and they are controlled by remote."

"Nice," she said with a nod as she continued on a self-guided tour through the first floor of the house. She brushed her hand across the back of one of the sofas in the open floor area. "Who designed your place?"

Ian pretended to look insulted. "You don't think I could have designed my own place?"

Giselle smiled at him and shook her head. "You're cute."

"Izzy," he said, referring to his sister.

"I knew it," Giselle said, triumphantly.

"Come on," he said, heading for the kitchen. He hit the light to one of his favorite places in the house. He noticed the impressed look on Giselle's face as she sat down on one of the bar stools.

"I don't think I've seen a house quite like yours, Ian," Giselle said as he opened his Sub-Zero refrigerator.

"It's made out of shipping containers," he said absently, as he pulled items out of the fridge.

"Shut up!"

"It's true," he said, placing several vegetables on the island before turning to grab some steaks. "I had it built about three years ago."

"It's amazing."

"Wait until you see the rest of the house."

"Are you referring to the bedroom?"

Ian looked at Giselle before he reached up and grabbed a pan from the hanging pot rack.

"I wasn't specifically talking about the bedroom," he said with a grin. "Get you mind out of the gutter."

Giselle laughed and then said, "So, what made you go with a container home."

"They're cost effective and eco-friendly," Ian said, as he lightly drizzled olive oil in the pan and turned on the stove burner.

"So, Ian Noble is all about saving the environment," Giselle asked.

"We only get one Earth."

"Anything I can do to help?" Giselle offered as Ian seasoned the steaks.

"Sure," he said. He pointed to a cabinet. "Grab a bowl from out of the there and you can put the salad together."

She went to the sink, washed and dried her hands and then grabbed the bowl. She pulled a knife out of the block on the counter and began to chop the tomatoes for the salad. Ian grinned when she popped a slice into her mouth and moaned.

"This is the freshest tomato I've ever tasted."

"They better be, they were pulled from my garden yesterday."

"You have a garden too?" Giselle asked.

Ian nodded as he picked the steaks up one at a time and placed them on the skillet.

"How do you like your steak?"

"Medium well."

"I actually have a greenhouse out back," Ian said. "One of the reasons I bought this place is because of the land. I wanted to have my own sustainable food system."

"You don't have cows and chickens out there too, do you?"

Ian smiled as he kept a close eye on the steaks. "No, but I only buy grass fed steaks and pasture-based meats."

"You've mostly been in Vegas, so who takes care of this?"

"I have hired help. But my mom likes to come as well. But mostly to 'shop'."

"I would too."

"I have more than enough, you're welcome to anything you want."

"What all do you have?"

Ian began calling off all of the fruits and vegetables he had growing in the greenhouse.

"I just might take you up on your offer."

Giselle continued working on the salad as Ian flipped the steaks over.

"So," he said. "How did Giselle the aerialist come to fruition?"

"I was wondering when you were going to bring that up."

"You knew I would."

She finished the salad and took it over to the dining area table, sneaking another tomato.

"I took an aerial yoga class a few years ago and loved it so much that I looked more into aerial arts. I took some of those classes as well and got hooked. I'm actually a certified aerial yoga teacher as well."

"Yeah?" Ian asked, impressed.

"I teach at the yoga studio in town a few nights a week."

He'd love to see that. But he was still looking forward to a private show from her.

"And Gyspy? How did she end up performing at Joie de Burlesque?"

"I worked there through college."

"Oh really?" Ian asked, raising an eyebrow as he plated the steaks.

"Not like *that*," she said, slapping him on the arm. "Though there isn't anything wrong with what they're doing."

"I agree. It's art."

"Damn right it is."

"What did you do there while you were in college?"

"I started off as a waitress during my undergrad years. After I turned twenty-one, I started working as a bartender, while I earned my master's."

"So, you have some skills in mixing up drinks?"

"I mean...I do all right," she said with a grin.

"Show me what you've got," Ian said.

"What kind of liquor do you have to mix up?"

He walked over to a large cabinet and opened it, revealing all kind of spirits and mixes, along with a full set of bar tools.

"Pick your poison," Ian said.

Giselle perused the bottles for a few moments and then grabbed a couple of bottles.

"I haven't done this in ages," she said, removing her jacket and rolling up the sleeves of her top. "I need an orange and a knife."

Ian grabbed the items she requested as she filled two martini glasses with ice. His eyes grew wide as he watched Giselle take one of the liquor bottles and flip it in the air, catching it by the neck as she poured it into the tin cup. She grabbed the other bottle she'd picked up, tossed it behind her and it came up and over her shoulder. It bumped her elbow before she caught it and tipped it into the cup with the other liquor.

She stirred the drink, poured the ice out and filled both

glasses with the concoction. She cut the rind off of the orange and used it as garnish on the drinks. She handed Ian, who was still awestruck by the flair tricks she'd done, one of the glasses.

"What was all that fancy shit you just did?"

Giselle laughed. "That fancy shit was what I learned working the bar at Joie de Burlesque. They never simply serve drinks."

That was true, Ian thought. Even getting a drink at the bar was a show.

"Taste it," Giselle insisted.

"What is this?" he asked.

"It's called 'the Hanky Panky'," she said, wiggling her eyebrows.

Ian took a sip. "Wow, that's strong. Are you trying to get me drunk, Miss Warren?"

"Maybe," she teased. "Come on, let's eat."

Chapter Sixteen

As usual, Ian's food was spectacular.

Giselle made them a few more drinks and showed off a few more of her old bartender tricks, claiming she was rusty, but Ian shut those comments down quickly.

"I couldn't do anything like that."

"Sure you could," she said. "They're actually easier than you'd think once you learn the basics. I could show you."

Ian shook his head. "I've had too much to drink tonight to be trying to toss bottles around. I'll just have to take your word for it," he said.

They were relaxing on the couch in front of the fire Ian had lit. His house was on a higher elevation, so it got much cooler at night, even in the warmer seasons. Giselle had gotten rid of her shoes a long time ago and her feet were tucked underneath her body.

"How was lunch with your family?"

"It was good, it was nice talking to my sisters." It had to be bittersweet, Giselle thought.

"Oh and I forgot to ask last week, how was the brunch with your mother?" she asked.

"It was good, better than I expected," Ian said.

"How so?" she asked before she took a sip of the latest drink she'd mixed up for them. She was beginning to feel a slight buzz.

"My manager called while I was there."

"What did he–"

"She," Ian corrected.

"What did *she* say?"

"She said that I should be able to go back to the restaurant after my suspension is over with no problem. In fact, they say they can't wait."

"That's great," Giselle said, smiling at him. She studied his face. "It's great right? You don't seem like you're excited about it?"

Ian sighed and turned to stare at the fire.

"Can I tell you something, Gi?"

"Of course, you know you can tell me anything with no judgement, Ian."

"I'm tired of the restaurant."

"You're tired of cooking?" Giselle asked surprised.

"No...I'm not tired of cooking. I'm just tired of the hustle and bustle of working at a restaurant."

"So what was so good about the phone call if you're not looking forward to going back to work now?"

His eyes sparkled a bit when he turned back to her. "I've been talking to some producers at CookNetwork about getting my own TV show. I thought after...the incident, I blew my chances out of the water. But it turns out, they're still interested."

"So that's what you want to do? Host your own cooking show?"

"Yeah," Ian said. "Even though it was rough sometimes, I had a great time on the competition show. And I've got so many things I'd like to be sharing with the people."

"I think you'd be great with your own show."

"Yeah?" he asked.

"Yeah."

There was something about the boyish grin he gave her. It showed a small bit of vulnerability in him and she felt special that only she got to see it.

"Where would you do your show?" she asked.

The smile slipped from his face slightly.

"I don't really know. It could be Vegas, or maybe L.A."

"Either way, you'll be leaving."

"Most likely."

Giselle nodded, annoyed by the ache in her chest at the thought of him leaving.

"You okay, Gi?"

"I'm fine," she said, forcing a smile.

She finished off her drink, sat the glass down on the coffee table and stood. "Show me the rest of the house."

"Okay," he said, standing as well.

They went upstairs and down the long hallway. He opened several doors, showing her each room. When they reached the end of the hallway, Ian opened the door and let Giselle walk in first.

Like every other room in the house, there were more windows than walls. The focal point of the room, of course, was the California king bed in the center of the room against the grey tufted upholstered headboard.

Giselle walked over to the bed and brushed her fingers against the soft down comforter. "I'll bet this..." she said, pointing to the bed. "Has been a huge selling point for the ladies."

Ian rocked back on his heels. "No other woman's seen my house here in Sweet Rapids."

Giselle turned and looked at him in disbelief. "Get out of town."

"I'm almost there," he joked.

"How is it that no other woman has seen 'the Great Ian Noble's bedroom'?" Giselle teased.

She watched as his lip tilted up slightly.

"This place is something I consider a sanctuary. I don't let just anyone into my inner sanctum. It's too private."

Giselle walked over to the window and looked out. It was pitch black outside and she couldn't see a thing.

"I've asked you this before, but I have to ask again," Giselle said. "Why me?"

She saw his reflection in the window moving toward her. He wrapped his strong arm around her waist and pulled her against him. She felt his hard length against her lower back and she was tempted to roll her body against it.

"I feel a connection with you that I've never felt with any other woman. It both fascinates me and scares the living shit out of me at the same time. I can't explain it, but I also know I can't deny it."

Her head fell back against his shoulder and he lowered his head to kiss her lips. Her eyes drifted closed and she felt his fingers going to work on unbuttoning her blouse. She let the shirt fall off of her shoulders to the floor and she turned to face him.

Giselle's hands went to Ian's pants as he pulled his shirt over his head. In no time, he stood in front of her completely naked. She licked her lips in anticipation of what was about to happen. He spun her around again and undid the hooks of her bra.

Her hands flew to the window when she felt his lips on her spine. She watched him through the window as he dropped to his knees behind her and reached around to undo her slacks, while he pressed his lips to her waist. He slid them down slowly, kissing and gently biting her hips, her ass and her legs all the way down to her calves. She stepped out of the pants and Ian tossed them out of the way. He stood again, and she heard the rustling of a wrapper. A moment later his body engulfed hers again as he pulled her away from the window. One hand went to her breasts, teasing and tantalizing her nipples; while the other hand spread the lips between her legs.

"Look at yourself," Ian whispered into her ear.

Giselle opened her eyes and she noticed Ian watching them as well. Her breast heaved as he fondled them with one hand, while her pussy vibrated with need against the other.

"You are so fucking beautiful, Giselle," he said, before his teeth gently sank into her shoulder.

She moaned loudly, enjoying the slight pain of his teeth, followed by the pleasure of the soothing kisses he planted there.

Giselle continued watching Ian through the window. He couldn't keep his hands or mouth off of her body, and she wanted to touch him as well. She reached behind her and wrapped one of her hands around his dick. His arm tightened around her body when she began to stroke him.

"Shit," he breathed through clenched teeth.

Giselle slid her other hand between her own legs and joined in with Ian's ministrations and he swore again.

They kept at it for several minutes until Ian grabbed her arms and splayed them out wide against the window again. She braced herself, as much as she could, as he bent her over slightly, lifted her up from behind and slid inside of her. Her feet nearly dangled off the floor, but his grip on her thighs were like a vise as he stroked her long and strong.

She was on the brink of coming when he pulled out. She glared at him over her shoulder and was about to ask him what he was doing, when he tossed her into his arms and carried her to the bed.

He placed her in the center, climbed on top of her and entered her again.

Her nails dug into his shoulders as he pounded in and out of her over and over, causing her to scream his name.

As Giselle came undone, Ian continued, his own climax on its way.

"Giselle," he growled, before slamming into her one last time.

She kept her eyes closed for several minutes as she tried to catch her breath. She could feel the rise and fall of Ian's chest against hers as he did the same. She opened them when she felt him push her curls out of her face.

"You're doing something to me, Gi," he whispered. His eyes were filled with both confusion and wonder.

She reached up and caressed his cheek, and he kissed her palm.

"You're doing something to me too, Ian."

Chapter Seventeen

Ian lightly traced the tattoo of two monarch butterflies intertwined in an orange ribbon on Giselle's shoulder. He'd been up half the night watching her sleep.

She shifted under his touch and rolled on to her side.

"Hey," she said, her voice sexy and filled with sleep.

"Hey." His hand was still on her shoulder and she looked back at it.

"What's the deal behind the tattoo?" he asked. He wasn't surprised that she had one; he'd been turned on even more at the sight of it the night before when he was undressing her from behind. He was just curious about it.

Giselle sighed, and Ian caught the hint of sadness in her eyes. "Another story for another day," she said somberly, as she sat up in bed and stretched.

The tattoo must have held some significance to it that she wasn't quite ready to talk about.

"But you'll tell me about it one day?"

"One day..." she promised, with a small smile. "But I need to get out of here. I have to go home and get ready for work."

She rolled away from him, got out of bed and padded

across the room. She didn't bother trying to cover herself and he loved how comfortable she was in her own skin. Ian watched as she picked her clothes up that were scattered across the room. She stood up and looked over at him, the sun rising behind her through the window.

The things he'd done to her against that window, before carrying her to the bed...

She smiled at him, as if she remembered the same thing, and then she ducked off to the bathroom.

He was tempted to follow her in there, but he knew they'd both be late for work if he did that, so he stayed in the bed until she came out several minutes later, fully dressed again.

She headed toward him and crawled back on to the large bed toward him. She pressed her lips to his in a long lingering kiss.

"Last night was amazing," she said.

"It was," he agreed, wrapping his hands around her, cupping her bottom. His lips found her neck and he kissed her until she began to squirm and push herself away from him.

"Ian, I have to go."

Reluctantly, he dropped his hands away.

"I'll see you in a few hours," she said.

"Do you want me to walk you out?" he asked.

She shook her head. "I can manage on my own."

He watched as she turned and left the bedroom. He heard the front door open and close and then he heard Giselle's car start and drive off.

He stayed in the bed for a bit longer and then finally got up. He got his clothes ready for work, and then went to shower and shave. After he got dressed, he made himself a quick breakfast before heading off to work.

By the time he got there, Giselle was arriving as well. They usually got to Noble Naturals headquarters early. But today, they arrived right on time.

He held the door open for Giselle as she walked into the building.

"Good morning," he murmured.

"It is a good morning indeed," she responded.

Once they were on the elevator, his eyes cut to her and he noticed the hint of a smile playing on her lips.

"Hold the elevator."

Ian's fist balled as Thomas rushed and joined them on the elevator. Ian and Giselle moved to opposite ends of the elevator. Thomas stood in front of them.

"Good morning, Giselle," Thomas said over his shoulder in her direction.

"Good morning," she replied.

"Noble," he said, addressing Ian.

"Walsh."

The elevators slid shut, filling the small compartment with tension. Ian's eye caught Giselle's again and he winked at her, causing her cheeks to heat.

They reached their floor and the doors opened. Thomas went out first and Ian stood back so Giselle could exit before him. He watched the sway of her ass and remembered all of the things they'd done the night before.

"Is everybody ready to work?" Giselle asked everyone in the lab. "Tomorrow's a big day."

She received affirmative nods from the other co-workers, including Ian. She had a nervous, yet excited energy radiating off of her body.

"Great," she said. "Let's get to work."

Ian glanced over at Giselle, who was fidgeting next to him. It was an interesting sight-seeing a woman, who appeared to be completely unbothered about everything, nervous. He watched her mouth moving and he could hear the sound of the ball of her tongue ring, rolling across her teeth.

Since working with her for nearly three months, he'd noticed that she usually did this habit when she was deep in thought. Apparently, she did it when she was uneasy as well.

Ian turned back to look through the observation window and watched the test subjects as they used the new Noble Naturals products. Several other employees from the lab were in the room; Isaiah and Irene were present as well.

He knew she was apprehensive because she wanted so badly for things to go well. He wanted things to go well too; and not just for the improvement of his family's company, but because Giselle wanted it. And if Giselle wanted something, Ian wanted to make it happen.

Giselle blew out a long, tense breath. Her fingers tapped furiously against her thigh; another habit of hers. He reached out, took her hand in his and interlocked their fingers. The rolling of her tongue ring stopped and out of his peripheral, he noticed her look down at their intertwined hands.

He felt her body relax instantly. They sat for the next hour watching testers try out several of their products. He never let go of her hand.

"That went well," Isaiah said, once the trial was over.

"I agree," Irene said.

"We'll check out the testers' written assessments, but judging from what was said in there, I think we're on the right track with the new products. Good job everyone," Isaiah said to everyone in the room, his gaze landing on Ian and Giselle last.

"Thank you, Isaiah," Giselle said.

Irene looked at her watch. "It's almost quitting time, you all go ahead and take the rest of the day off, you've earned it."

After everyone filed out of the observation room, Ian turned to Giselle. He let out a grunt as she threw her body against his, flinging her arms around his neck. He chuckled and squeezed his arms around her waist.

"You did it, Gi," he said.

She pulled away and shook her head. "*We* did it, Ian."

He kicked the door closed, pressed Giselle against it and leaned down to kiss her. She responded instantly, her grip around his neck tightening. He pulled away and noticed her eyes glittering with excitement.

"Come on," he said, pulling the door open.

"Where are we going?" she laughed, as he tugged her along.

"To celebrate."

Giselle groaned, her head pounding from an obvious hangover. She opened her eyes and quickly shut them again, the light too much to handle. She brushed her wild hair out of her face.

Slowly, she opened her eyes again and they grew wide with alarm. Finally taking in her surroundings, she realized she was in a hotel room.

Why was she in a hotel room?

She brought her hand up to her temples to try and stave off the throbbing. Her heart dropped into her stomach when her eyes caught sight of her fingers.

More specifically, the *ring* on her left hand.

"What the fuck!" she gasped.

Quickly, she looked around and noticed Ian's naked body lying beside her in the bed. Her right wrist was in a handcuff, connected to Ian's left.

"Oh my god...*Ian!*" she shouted.

He groaned and shifted but didn't do much else so she shoved her foot into his side, nearly kicking him off of the bed.

"Shit," he growled. "What the hell, Gi?"

"'What the hell' is right!" she said. Ian looked around the room, confused and then he lifted his cuffed wrist, causing a smile to spread across his face. His amused grin faded quickly when he saw the newest accessory on his finger. His head jerked up and his eyes, filled with shock, locked with Giselle's.

"We..." He shook his head. "No. No, no, no, no!"

Giselle, who was on the brink of hyperventilating, held up her hand.

"Ian...what did we do?"

"Holy sh–"

Chapter Eighteen

"Shit, shit, shit..."

Giselle had been swearing for the last few minutes, while Ian tried to clear his foggy brain. The previous night was a huge blur. The last thing he remembered was driving to Reno with Giselle to celebrate the first round of tests going well with the new Noble Naturals products.

They ended up going to several bars and obviously having way too many shots of tequila.

"There's no way," he murmured. He looked over at Giselle. "We wouldn't have."

"Obviously we did," Giselle snapped while holding their handcuffed wrists up to show him the stark reminder on his finger.

"We...we got *married*?" he whispered.

Giselle shot up out of the bed, causing Ian's body to jerk forward.

"Giselle!"

"Where the hell is the key to these things?"

He yanked on the handcuffs and she fell back on the bed.

"Can you chill for a minute?" he said. "And stop yelling." He grabbed his throbbing forehead with his free hand.

Giselle whipped her head in his direction. It was then that he realized she had a short veil pinned to her hair. She snatched it off and chunked it to the floor.

"Chill?" she said. "Ian...we got drunk and got married! And you're saying chill?"

"Yes," he said, surprised by how freakishly calm he was. "It's not a big deal, Gi. This is Nevada; people do things like this all the time. When Monday gets here, we'll go to the courthouse and get it annulled."

Giselle began to calm down, listening to Ian's reasoning. "Right," she said, nodding her head. "We'll just get it annulled." She looked down at the handcuffs. "Looks like we had one hell of a honeymoon."

Ian chuckled. "I'm glad we can find *some* humor in this situation. Let's find that key, now."

They stood together and searched around the room, eventually finding the key. Ian unlocked the handcuffs and they both rolled their wrists, thankful to be free.

They got cleaned up and had just finished getting dressed when a loud pounding on the door caught them by surprise.

Giselle looked at him confused. "Did you order room service?"

Ian shook his head, and then cringed when the banging started back up, followed by shouting.

"Ian Noble! Open this fucking door!"

"Shit," he whispered.

"Who is that?" Giselle asked.

"My damn publicist," he groaned, trudging to the door.

He opened it and Michelle stormed in.

"Chelle–"

"Stay out of trouble. That's what I said, isn't it?" she asked.

"*All* you had to do was lay low for a few months and...Stay. Out. Of. Trouble!"

"And I have–"

"And then guess what I see on the social media sites this morning?"

Ian eyes fell shut and his head dropped.

"'Celebrity Chef Ian Noble Gets Hitched in Reno!'"

"How'd you even know I was here?" he asked.

"I am your manager, Ian. It is my *job* to know where you are and what you are doing at all times. Although you make it ridiculously difficult sometimes." Michelle blew out a breath. "The producers are coming the day after tomorrow to discuss concept ideas for your cooking show. They're going to want an explanation."

She was now pacing, which meant she was in 'damage control mode'.

"Although they've still been interested in you, they have been concerned about your 'bad boy' image. Most of their shows are watched by families..."

Michelle froze and turned to look at Ian and Giselle.

"Chelle?" Ian said, not sure he liked the look on her face.

"You two work together, right?"

"Yes," Ian said. There was no point in asking her how she knew. Like she said, it was her business to know.

"That's crazy enough that it just might work," Michelle said to herself.

"*What* is crazy enough that it just might work?"

"You two have to stay married."

Giselle's mouth fell open.

Ian blinked and looked at his manager as if she'd just grown a second head.

"Michelle," he said, slowly. "Are you out of your mind?"

"Face it, Ian. Your image desperately needs revamping. Despite *how* you ended up getting married, this could still work in our favor. If we project to the people that Ian Noble has 'suddenly found love' and it's changed you for the better, the network will eat it up."

Michelle started pacing again, obviously pleased with her idea.

"We could even convince them to let you do the show at your home in Sweet Rapids."

Ian shook his head. "The plan has always been to do a show in Vegas or L.A."

"But they'll love seeing you in your natural element, with your whole garden to table system, and your greenhouse..."

Ian looked at Giselle, who appeared to be as flabbergasted as he was, as Michelle kept talking and planning. She hadn't said a word since Michelle came into the hotel room.

"Wait a minute," Ian said, holding his hands up. "Nobody's agreeing to this, Chelle. Giselle and I just had *way* too much to drink last night and things got out of hand. Monday morning we're going to the courthouse–"

"And you'll be all over the tabloids...*again*. This time, they'll be going on and on about your forty-eight hour marriage and how, along with being a home wrecking philanderer, you also can't hold your liquor."

Michelle's words were harsh, but true.

Ian ran a hand down his face. "Look, I see your point. But this isn't just my life you're talking about completely altering."

"You could stay married for a year or so. After that, you could split amicably." Michelle turned and addressed Giselle for the first time. "We could pay you, if that's what you want."

"Michelle," Ian thundered, instantly pissed off at her offer. "Do not speak to her like that."

"We have to be realistic about this situation, Ian," Michelle shouted back.

Michelle and Ian began going back and forth arguing when Giselle's voice suddenly broke through the noise.

"I'll do it."

Both Ian and Michelle turned to Giselle.

"What?" Ian said.

"I'll stay married to you."

Giselle stood in the middle of the hotel room staring at Ian, who had a shocked expression on his face.

"Gi–"

"Good," Michelle said, pulling out her cellphone. "We can get you a check after we discuss–"

"No," Giselle said quickly.

Michelle looked up Giselle confused. "No?"

"I don't want your money," she said, making sure to look directly at Ian when she said those words.

Ian moved to stand in front of Giselle. He stopped mid-stride and turned to look at Michelle. She raised her eyebrow at him and he shot her an annoyed look.

"Can you give us a damn minute?"

Michelle turned and walked toward the bedroom of the suite, closing the door to give Ian and Giselle some privacy.

He reached out and cupped Giselle's cheek. "I can't ask you to do this. It's my mess. I can't drag you into all of this."

Giselle shook her head. "You didn't get drunk and married by yourself, Ian. We made this particular mess together. And your manager's right. The last thing you need right now is more bad publicity. You've just had an unlucky streak when it comes to the media. You're not really how they portray you."

"There *has* to be another option."

"On such short notice? Michelle said the producers are coming the day after tomorrow and they've already heard we're married." She reached up and took his hand. "I *know* how much you want this show. Michelle's idea makes the most sense in order to get what you want right now. You don't want them thinking you're reckless and irresponsible, because you're far from that."

Ian still looked unconvinced, so she squeezed his hand. "We can do this, Ian."

"Are you *sure* about this, Giselle? Maybe you should take a few days to think–"

"You don't have a few days," she said. "I'm in."

He pulled her to him and kissed her. He pressed his forehead to hers. "There's no way I could properly thank you for this."

"Oh, I'm going to cash in every chance I can get," she teased.

She took a step back, but he grabbed her by the wrist.

"This is huge," he said.

"I'm aware of that."

"Whenever you decide you're tired of this situation, when you're ready to...bow out...just say the word."

Giselle nodded, unable to speak.

What the hell are you doing, her head screamed. But her heart felt like it was the right thing to do. Ian was a good person; he'd just had bad luck when it came to the media.

"Chelle," Ian called out.

The French doors swung open and Michelle came back into the living room.

"What's the plan?" Ian sighed.

"We'll send out a press release, letting the media know that you kept your relationship private and you'd appreciate it if they respect your desire for it to remain that way."

Ian nodded. "And the meeting on Monday?"

"When they bring up your marriage, which they will, we'll give them some short and sweet answer about how you two fell hard and fast and didn't want to waste time being apart. We'll sidetrack them by giving them a tour of your house, and the grounds. I'm going to present them with the idea of you doing the cooking show from your home, showing your 'warmer side'. We may even suggest featuring your new bride on a few episodes."

"Fine," Ian said. "Do what you need to do."

Michelle nodded and headed for the door.

"I'll make arrangements to have your things moved to Ian's place, Giselle."

"Moved?" Giselle asked.

Michelle stopped and turned. "Of course. You're Mrs. Ian Noble now. If you're *really* agreeing to this, that means you're putting yourself out there for the media's scrutiny. You can't very well be seen going in and out of your apartment all of the time, while Ian lives at his house."

"Are you still sure about this?" Ian asked.

Giselle nodded before she lost her nerve.

"I'll get the ball rolling," Michelle said.

After Michelle left, Giselle sat down on the sofa in the living room area of the suite.

The sound of Giselle's ringtone from her phone filled the air, followed by Ian's phone. He pulled his phone out of his pocket and swore.

"My brother's calling."

"Damn," Giselle whispered, realization slamming through her.

How was she going to explain this to her family?

Chapter Nineteen

Giselle blew out a fortifying breath and she returned the most important call she'd been ignoring for the last hour as she and Ian worked out a plan.

"Hi, Daddy."

"GiGi," Russell Warren's strong voice came through the speakerphone. She breathed a sigh of relief at the comforting tone. But that's just how her father was; always calm and collected no matter what kind of trouble his youngest daughter got into. "It seems congratulations are in order."

"Yes, sir."

"How are you?"

"I'm good, Daddy."

"And this Noble guy?"

Giselle looked over at Ian. "He's a great guy."

"Are you happy?"

"Of course I am."

Russell blew out a breath. "I'd be lying if I said I didn't like the way you've gone about this. But you're an adult and you've always been a bit unconventional."

"That's for sure."

"So as long as you're happy, that's what's most important. But I want to meet this young man."

"You will, Daddy. And thank you. I love you."

"I love you too."

"Is that GiGi?"

Giselle sighed at the sound of her mother's voice in the background. Talking to her mother wasn't going to go as smoothly as talking to her father had been.

"Sophia..." Russell said in a warning tone to her mother.

"Give me the phone," Sophia ordered. A moment later, her mother's voice filled the phone. "Giselle Tania Warren! How could you?"

Giselle rolled the ball of her tongue ring against her teeth. She stopped when she felt Ian take her hand and give it a gentle squeeze.

"Mommy," Giselle said in a soothing voice. She tried reiterating her father's logic on the whole ordeal. "You know I've never done anything traditional."

"But getting married in *Vegas!*"

"Reno, Mommy. We got married in Reno."

"Same difference. The point is how could you just run off and get married like that and not tell us?"

Giselle glanced over at Ian who was driving. They were headed to his mother's house to have the same conversation.

"It all happened so fast," Giselle said.

"That's just it," Sophia said. "Sometimes you jump the gun on these types of things. Let's not forget the young man you fell for in college and he landed you in jail."

Giselle's eyes rolled and her head fell back against the headrest. The car came to a stop at a red light and she felt Ian's curious gaze on her.

"I haven't forgotten about that," she said. "This is...different."

That part she didn't have to lie about.

"I don't know GiGi–"

Giselle looked around confused when Ian pulled off to the side of the road, parked and took the phone from Giselle's hand.

"Mrs. Warren," Ian said in his deep, smooth voice.

"Umm...yes?"

Was her mother actually breathless?

"This is Ian Noble."

"I've seen you on TV." Why did her mother sound all giddy now? "I was rooting for you."

"And I appreciate that," he said, his smile on the highest level as if Sophia could see it. "I apologize for the way you found out about how Giselle and I got married. As you know, I'm often followed by the paparazzi, even when I'm unaware."

"That must be such a burden, dear."

"It comes with the territory. But I just want you to know that my feelings for your daughter are real. And I just couldn't go another day without making her my wife. I was lucky enough that she felt the same way about me."

Silence filled the phone for a brief moment and Giselle held her breath. Finally her mother sighed and said, "That's *so* romantic."

Giselle looked up at Ian in shock and he winked at her.

"I'm going to do everything in my power to continuing showering your daughter with everything she wants and needs for the rest of our lives."

"Make sure you do. Our GiGi has been through so much."

"I assure you she's in good hands, Mrs. Warren." The naughty grin Ian gave Giselle nearly made her blush. The things he did to her with his hands...and his mouth...and–

"Oh! We're family now. You can call me, Mom," Sophia said.

"Mommy, we have to go," Giselle called out, still in disbelief at what Ian had just pulled off with his mother. "We're on our way to see Ian's mother. Let CiCi know I'll call her soon," Giselle said.

"Okay, dear. We love you."

"Love you too."

Giselle hung up the phone, looked up at Ian and grinned.

"Oh, you're good."

Ian put his shades on and put the car in drive.

"I'm the best, baby," he said, before hitting the gas and taking off to his mother's house.

Ian pulled into the driveway of his mother's home and took off his shades.

"You okay?"

He looked over at Giselle and smiled. "I'm fine, jailbird."

"Ugh, you're not going to stop with that, are you?"

"Nope, or the fact that you still call your mother 'mommy'."

"*Lots* of people do that," Giselle argued.

On the drive to Noble Estates, Ian had teased Giselle relentlessly.

"It's just nice to know we're two peas in a criminal pod."

"Shut up."

The front door swung open and Irene stepped out onto the porch. Isaiah and Tessa were standing behind her, holding hands.

"I guess we should get this over with."

"Is this going to be better or worse than my parents?" Giselle asked.

He looked at his mother's face, but as usual, the older woman's expression was unreadable.

"I can't tell," Ian admitted. He opened his car door, went

around and opened Giselle's door and took her hand. "You ready for this?"

"As ready as I'm gonna get."

Ian shut the door, turned and they walked up the porch steps.

"Mom," Ian said, looking down at her.

She studied them for a moment, and then her eyes filled with tears.

Shit.

"I'm sorry," Irene said, covering her mouth. "But I just *knew* she was the one for you."

Ian peeked over at Giselle, who visibly swallowed.

"I just wish your father was alive to see this," his mother added.

This time, Ian swallowed, trying not to let the guilt of their facade overtake him. Both Ian and Giselle were surprised when Irene rushed forward and pulled them both into a warm hug.

"I'm so happy for the two of you," she said. She stepped back and gave them a stern glare. "Although, I have to be honest, I wasn't thrilled at how I found out or the fact that you just ran off and did this quickie ceremony."

"We're sorry about that, Mom. We just didn't want the whole big wedding shindig."

"I suppose I can understand that. Your father and I got married at the courthouse. However, you have to let me throw you the most amazing reception."

"Mom–" Ian started.

"This is not up for discussion. It's the least you can let me do for the two of you."

Ian looked at Giselle and she smiled at Irene. "We would love that, Miss Irene. Thank you."

Irene grabbed Giselle's arm and led her into the house. "Your family must come as well," she insisted.

"Dana and I can make the cake or desserts," Tessa added, joining Irene and Giselle.

Once the women were out of earshot, gabbing about plans for the reception, Isaiah turned to Ian.

"Now that Mom's gone, you wanna cut the bullshit and tell me what *really* happened?"

Ian moved to one of the rocking chairs, and Isaiah closed the front door for privacy, before joining Ian by sitting in the chair across from him.

"Long story short...too much tequila."

"Nah," Isaiah said, shaking his head. "You've gotta give me more than that."

Ian let his head fall against the chair. "A lot has happened in the last twenty-four hours. Shit, I'm still hungover to be honest. Michelle found us and came through like the pit bull she can be–"

"To do what she could to save your ass. Again."

"I meant it as a compliment," Ian said. "She was in full 'fix-it' mode."

"I can tell," Isaiah said. "She had a press release out before you guys even got here."

"She's the best for a reason."

"Back to you and Giselle though," Isaiah pressed.

Ian shut his eyes, trying to remember the events from the night before.

"We left work after Mom said take the rest of the day off. Gi was so happy that the initial trials went well, I decided that we should go out and celebrate."

Isaiah nodded. "That sounds normal enough. How do you go from celebrating accomplishments at work to celebrating nuptials?"

Ian squinted his eyes. "I vaguely remember after, I don't know what number drink it was, I think we were talking about our parents and how they were married for so long. I think I said something about probably never being able to settle down. I think she said something about how she'd marry me in a heartbeat. I *might* have actually gotten down on one knee in the bar. There were a couple of rides in a limo, and more drinking..."

Isaiah leaned closer to Ian and lowered his voice. "Are you sure you're *actually* married? I mean, yeah, you went to the chapel, but you have to have–"

"A marriage license?" Ian finished, as he reached into his pocket. He pulled out a folded piece a paper from the envelope and passed it to over to Isaiah. He watch as Isaiah unfolded it and read it. "I told you there were a couple of rides in the limo. One of which was obviously to the marriage license bureau, followed by a trip to the drive through chapel before we ended up back at the hotel."

"What does Giselle remember about last night?"

"About as much as I do," Ian said.

"Holy shit," Isaiah mumbled, still looking at the marriage license Ian and Giselle had found earlier that morning as they'd been searching for the key to the handcuffs. "You're fucking married."

"I'm fucking married," Ian repeated.

"But...why are you *staying* married?" Isaiah asked. "What's with the whole, 'respect our privacy' press release Michelle put out and this act you're putting on for Mom like you're blissfully in love and happy."

Ian looked up at the porch ceiling. "Chelle thinks that showing the world that I'm now a happily married man will help clean up my image."

"And Giselle went along with it?"

Ian smiled at the thought of her and how she was coming through for him. "Yeah, she did. I must have done something right to deserve such an amazing fake wife."

"According to this paper," Isaiah said, waving it in the air. "There's nothing fake about her being your wife."

"I guess you're right."

Both men sat on the porch in silence for a few minutes before Isaiah chuckled, "You're fucking married!"

"Yeah...I'm fucking married."

Chapter Twenty

By the time Ian and Giselle left his mother's house, it was late in the afternoon. As a 'wedding gift', she'd insisted they take the rest of the week off. They both tried to decline, but Irene wouldn't back down.

They were both exhausted and their hangovers were finally dissipating by the time they reached Ian's house. Michelle had sent Ian a text letting him know that the meeting with the network producers was still on for the next day and she ordered that both he and Giselle get plenty of rest so they could be at their best.

They drove back to Ian's place and collapsed on the sofa.

"Are you hungry?" Ian asked Giselle. "You barely ate any of the food Mom made for lunch."

Giselle covered her stomach and shook her head.

"It's just now settling down after last night's festivities."

Ian nodded his head in understanding. After sitting for a moment, he stood.

"What are you doing?" Giselle asked.

"I'm going to go and take a look around the greenhouse.

Make sure it looks good for tomorrow when we give the producers the tour out there."

"I'll come with you," she offered. "I've been wanting to see it ever since you told me about it."

"You should rest," Ian said. "It's been a long and overwhelming day. More so with my mother bombarding you with reception party talk."

He leaned down and kissed her on the forehead. "You'll get to see all of the grounds tomorrow."

Giselle looked as if she wanted to debate it, but instead she simply nodded and relaxed back on to the couch.

"I won't be long," Ian promised.

He went outside to the back of his house, opened the shed that held the utility vehicles he used to drive the quarter mile to the greenhouse. He got in one, started it and took off.

In no time, he arrived at the greenhouse. He went in, did a quick sweep of the place and nodded his head in approval. Between his mother and the hired help, they'd kept his fruits and vegetables thriving.

He planted his hand on one of the tables and blew out a breath. Anxiety over the events that occurred in the past twenty-four hours hit him square in the chest.

He was *married.* He still couldn't believe it.

Giselle, for all intents and purposes, was perfect. He thoroughly enjoyed spending time with her, in and out of bed.

But the fact remained, he barely knew this woman. He was still learning about her. And they'd agreed to stay married for the sake of his career.

Were they making a huge mistake? Could they *actually* pull off making the entire world believe they were this happy couple that just had to be together as husband and wife?

Ian wasn't so sure, but if Giselle was brave enough to give it a go, then dammit, he could man up and be brave too.

As his mini panic attack subsided, he left the greenhouse,

checked on a few more things and then got back in the vehicle and headed to the house.

When he went inside, he found Giselle still on the couch, but now she was sprawled out across it, lightly snoring.

He'd discovered she did that when she'd slept over several nights ago. He'd always thought little nuisances like that would annoy him, but surprisingly with Giselle, it didn't. He just found it oddly endearing.

He gently scooped her up into his arms and headed for the stairs. Her arms slid around his neck and her head rested on his shoulder. The scent of her hair wafted to his nostrils and he inhaled deeply, loving the scent of it as his nose brushed against the strands. It was now a dark brown and she had it styled in a super curly frohawk and it was as soft as a cloud.

She'd kicked her shoes off downstairs, so Ian placed her on the bed. She was wearing a dress, so he was able to easily undress her without disturbing her sleep. Fatigue seemed to set in and Ian stripped out of his clothes and climbed in bed with Giselle. He looked out the window in front of him watching the sun go down, as everything that had recently happened replayed in his head.

His eyes had just begun to drift close when he felt Giselle's ass snuggle into his side. He grew aroused instantly, but he was so exhausted that, for the first time in a long time, he desired sleep more than sex. But she felt too good to keep from touching her at all, so he rolled over, wrapped his arm around her waist and pulled her closer to his body.

He'd gone from never inviting a woman to his home in Sweet Rapids to having a new wife in his bed.

And the most insane thing about it all was...it felt right.

Giselle woke up with a start. She looked around, completely

disoriented. It took her a minute to realize she wasn't in her apartment. She was in Ian's bed.

Well, technically it was now *their* bed.

"It wasn't just a dream," she moaned.

"Nope, it wasn't just a dream."

She looked up to find Ian standing in the doorway with a tray in his hands.

"Good morning," he said, with a grin.

"Good morning." She looked at the clock on the nightstand. "We must have slept–"

"Over twelve hours," he finished.

"I don't think I've slept that much...in years."

"Me neither," Ian said, walking toward her with the tray of breakfast. "How are you feeling this morning?"

"Better than yesterday," she murmured, shaking her head.

Ian nodded. "That's good. Are you ready to do this today?"

"You mean play the part of your pretend wife."

"We have a piece of paper that says, according to the state of Nevada, that none of this is fake."

"You have a point there. But yes, I'm ready."

"I'll never be able to repay you for this, Gi. But at the very least, for now anyway, I can feed my new wife."

"How does it feel saying that? Your wife."

Ian's lip tilted up and that dimple that kicked her pulse up a notch showed itself. "It's going to take some getting used to. But...it's not bad."

He placed the tray in her lap and Giselle discovered, upon looking at the food, that she was a lot more hungry than she'd thought.

"French toast, scrambled eggs, bacon and orange juice," Ian said.

"It all looks delicious." She reached for the syrup when Ian suddenly grabbed her wrist stopping her.

"Wait," he said, quickly.

"What is it?" she asked, confused.

"You don't have any food allergies, do you? The syrup is maple pecan."

Giselle grinned and shook her head. "No food allergies."

"Good," Ian said. "Occupational habit, you could say."

"I appreciate the concern." She grabbed the knife and fork and then paused and looked at him. "Where's your plate?"

Ian shook his head. "I'm not that hungry."

"Ian, you made all of this food and you're not going to eat any?"

She knew he'd never admit it, but she could see the shadows of nervousness in his eyes. He'd caught a bad rap one too many times and he wanted this to go right this time around. She knew how important getting this television show was to him, which was why she'd selflessly gone along with staying married to him.

"Ian, you *have* to eat something. You can't present yourself to the producers on an empty stomach." She patted the bed next to her. "Come on, we can share this. There's no way I can eat it all by myself anyway."

Ian did something Giselle had never seen him do before, he hesitated. But it was brief, and a moment later, he was sitting on the bed next to her and they were sharing breakfast together.

After they were done eating, Giselle went and took a shower and got dressed, while Ian went downstairs to put the dishes away and clean up. They'd stopped by her apartment the day before on the way to Ian's house so she could pick up a few outfits. They'd be going back later in the week to pack up the rest of her things.

She wiped the fog away from the mirror and frowned at her hair, frustrated that she'd fallen asleep before she got a chance to do her nightly routine of moisturizing and twisting it before bed.

She was able to wrangle her hair into a cute puff before applying a light amount of makeup.

She was walking out of the master bathroom when Ian returned to the bedroom. He was fully dressed, looking handsome in his slacks, button down shirt, vest and tie.

His eyes took her in from head to toe before he spoke.

"You look amazing, Gi."

"Thank you. You look good too. Like you're ready to wow these people."

At that moment, the doorbell rang.

"I guess it's time to 'wow' them," Ian said.

Giselle moved toward him and reached up to fix his tie.

"Everything is going to go great," she assured him.

Ian nodded, gave her a quick kiss, and then took her hand in his and lead the way downstairs.

It was showtime.

Chapter Twenty-One

"I must say," Loreen Crawford, one of the network producers, said as she sat down. "We were quite shocked when we heard that you'd run off and gotten married. But looking at the two of you together..." She pressed her hand to her chest and sighed. "It's obvious why you didn't want to wait another moment."

"And I understand why you'd want to keep her all to yourself," Jim Porch, the other network producer, said. "Your wife is absolutely lovely."

Giselle dipped her head, in a show of modesty, before saying, "Thank you, Mr. Porch."

"Would you like some coffee?" Ian offered.

"Yes!" Loreen said. "It smells absolutely divine."

Giselle stood and grabbed the coffee pot and poured both Loreen and Jim a cup. "Did you know that Ian makes his own coffee blend?"

"Really?" Jim asked.

"Yes, sir," Ian said.

They each took a sip and looked at each other impressed.

"Well this is probably the best damn coffee I've ever tasted," Jim said.

"I thought the exact same thing when I first tried it," Giselle said as she sat back down next to Ian.

They did small talk for a few minutes while their guests finished their coffee and the pastries they'd gotten from Everetts', and then got down to business.

"We spoke to Michelle and she mentioned the idea of doing the show here at your home. Your garden to table platform is quite interesting," Loreen said.

"How about we head out to the greenhouse and I can show you around?" Ian offered.

"That sounds like a great idea."

They all got up, Ian taking Giselle's hand in his again and they led the way to the back.

"I love your home, Ian," Loreen exclaimed.

Ian thanked her and began to explain to her about how it was made out of shipping containers, and how a great deal of the home ran off of solar energy from the panels he had installed on the roof.

"This environmentally conscious side of you will play well with the audience, I think," Jim said.

"I hope so," Ian said, as he opened the shed. He pointed to a four-seater vehicle. "Let's hop in."

They all piled in and Ian drove them the short distance to the greenhouse. Giselle tried to hide the surprise as to how large it was. She'd been expecting something tiny, the size of a small shed perhaps. But Ian's greenhouse was just as big as his regular house.

"Oh my," Loreen said, voicing Giselle's shock. "Ian this is...amazing."

"Thank you," he said, as they got out. He went and opened the door and allowed everyone to go in before he followed them. "I try to grow as many fruits, vegetables and herbs here as possible. Since I've been in Vegas, I've had people come in and care for things, along with my mother. Of course I don't eat all of this myself, so a large portion of it is sold at local farmers markets throughout the county."

"Are those beekeeper suits?" Jim asked, pointing at the suits hanging on the wall.

"As a matter of fact they are," Ian said, pushing his hands into his pockets. "I also produce honey here and sell it locally."

Giselle couldn't stop her face from contorting into shock at that revelation.

"My my," Loreen said. "You certainly are a jack-of-all-trades, aren't you?"

"I just think that the best foods you can get are the foods you can produce yourself. Having your own sustainable food system helps with that tremendously. With so many preservatives and artificial ingredients that companies put into products these days, I believe it's best to stay as natural as possible. I learned that at a very early age."

"With your family's company," Jim pointed out. "Noble Naturals."

"Exactly," Ian said.

"Michelle also mentioned that you were working at Noble Naturals during your...off time from the restaurant in Vegas."

"That's true," Ian confirmed. "In college, I actually double majored in culinary science and chemistry. My two favorite things growing up. The culinary side has been in the forefront for so long, but Noble Naturals has recently begun revamping their company, which includes adding new products. When my brother asked me to help create some of the new lines, I couldn't say no. If I hadn't, I wouldn't have met this wonderful woman."

He pulled Giselle closer to him and kissed her cheek.

"So you work for Noble Naturals?" Loreen asked Giselle, her eyes sparkling.

Giselle nodded. "Yes ma'am."

"She's the head of the Production Department," Ian said, proudly. "Although we bumped heads about that, in the beginning."

"Really?"

"He needed an ego check," Giselle said, rolling her eyes and Loreen laughed.

"So it *wasn't* love at first sight?"

"No," both Ian and Giselle said at the same time and then smiled at each other.

"We did lock horns," Giselle said.

"But I got put in my place quickly," Ian conceded.

"The chemistry must have built quickly as well," Jim pondered

"After I extended an apology and an olive branch, we got along well," Ian said.

"And now you're married."

"Yes," Giselle said. "And now we're married."

"Jim, I think we've seen enough," Loreen said.

"I agree. Ian, we would love to get the ball rolling on a cooking show with you and CookNetwork."

Ian looked utterly shocked. "Are you serious?"

"Oh yes. After everything you've shown us today, we'd be foolish not to capitalize on it," Jim said. "It'll take a couple of months to get things worked out. But we'll be sending you a contract by the end of the week and we'll start hammering out when we can get your show into a viewing slot. You'll probably have to spend more time here is Sweet Rapids rather than in Vegas for production. Will that be a problem?"

"Not at all," Ian said, quickly. "I've enjoyed working at the restaurant over the last couple of years, but I'm definitely ready for something new."

"And so are we," Loreen said.

Ian extended his hand and shook Loreen's hand and then

Jim's hand. Both producers then turned to Giselle and they each shook her hand.

"You *must* join him on some episodes," Loreen insisted. "Your chemistry together is going to shoot the ratings through the roof."

"I'd be more than happy too," Giselle said.

They left the greenhouse and Ian drove them back to the house. Both Ian and Giselle stood in the doorway waving goodbye once Loreen and Jim got into their town car and drove off.

Ian shut the door, looked down at Giselle and then scooped her into his arms.

Giselle yelped at the sudden movement and then he kissed her deeply.

"I couldn't have done this without you, Giselle."

"Oh please," Giselle said. "You're Ian Noble, you would have done just fine without me."

"I can't believe it's happening."

"And I can't believe that greenhouse," she said. "That was out of this world! And you make your own honey. That's insane..."

"What?" he asked when the last of her words drifted off. She tilted her head to the side and studied him. "Why are you looking at me like that?"

She turned and went to the kitchen, muttering something under her breath over and over; and Ian followed her. He watched as she grabbed a pen and paper off of the counter and began scribbling.

"Oh...my...*goodness!*" Her head snapped up. "You're Abe Nilon!"

Abe Nilon was a locally sourced honey that was popular in the upper west region of Nevada.

"Abe Nilon," Giselle said again, picking up the bottle of honey sitting on the island. "It's an *anagram* for Ian Noble!"

"For some reason I'm finding you extremely hot right now," Ian said, with a grin as he moved toward her.

"I have this honey at home right now. It's the best."

"I'm glad you enjoy it," he said. He placed his hands on both sides of her on the island and Giselle looked around, realizing she was trapped.

"How..." Her breath hitched as his lips descended onto her neck. "How did you get into beekeeping?"

"Fourth grade field trip to a local farm," he murmured, as his lips moved down to her collar bone.

He took the honey from her hand and sat it on the counter.

"We'll use that later."

Her body shivered at the thought of him licking the honey off of her body. He grabbed the hem of her sundress pulled it over her head and tossed it aside before lifting her onto the long island. She watched as he stepped back, undressed and then climbed onto the island with her.

The marble countertop was cool on her back as she eased down on to it, while Ian's warm body hovered above her.

"You're wearing the underwear I bought you," he said, as his finger traced the waistband of her panties.

She could only nod, her body too keyed up now. It took little to no effort for Ian to fire her body up for him.

She lifted her hips as he pulled down the red, lace panties and then she spread her legs wide.

"I love the way you open up for me," he said in her ear as he slid inside of her. Once he filled her completely, he grabbed her legs and hooked them both over his shoulders. Changing positions seemed to make him go deeper inside of her and she moaned at the sensation. He pinned her wrists down to the island with his hands, leaving her helpless to do anything but hang on and enjoy the sensations of him plowing into her over and over.

Heat filled her belly as she felt an earth-shattering orgasm nearly split her in two. Her back bowed, and she knew that move brought on his own orgasm. He released her wrists and she removed her legs from his shoulders.

He planted his hands on the island so he wouldn't collapse on her.

As their breathing returned to normal, Giselle turned her head to the side and noticed the bottle of honey still next to their heads.

"We didn't get to use it," she said absently.

Ian grabbed the bottle and flicked the top open with his thumb.

"We can remedy that right now."

"So the meeting went well?" Ciara asked.

Giselle had finally taken the time to call her sister and fill her in on everything that had happened in the last forty-eight hours.

What had *really* happened. Not the bullshit press version Michelle had given the media, or what they'd told their parents to placate them.

She couldn't keep everything a secret from her big sister, and she needed someone to talk to, to figure out what was going on with her.

"Yes," she said, after sighing. "Everything went perfect. Ian did his thing and wowed the producers and I was the perfect new bride and hostess."

"I *still* can't believe you're married to Ian Noble."

"Yeah well, I've got the marriage license to prove it," she murmured. Her head fell forward into her free hand and she groaned. "CiCi, what am I doing here?"

"You're helping out a friend," she said.

"You make it seem so much simpler than the complicated mess it is."

"What's complicated about it?" Ciara asked. "You're friends, right?"

"I think we're more than that, at this point."

Not even an hour ago, he licked the honey he'd drizzled onto her body clean off.

"Don't be nasty," Ciara giggled. "My *point* is that you knew how it would make Ian look if you two got this thing annulled three days after running off, getting drunk and then getting married in Reno. You empathized with his plight and you did what you had to do to help him."

Giselle nodded, even though her sister couldn't see her. Hearing Ciara say those words validated what she was doing a little bit more.

"I have to admit though. I've been pretty tickled reading the comments on social media. Women are devastated that you've snatched him off the market," Ciara added.

Giselle had avoided the social media sites as much as possible.

"I'm not worried about any of that," she said.

"So what's next?" Ciara asked.

"We wait on the contract they're going to send Ian. They're actually eager to have me on the show as well." She didn't admit it out loud, but she was eager about that as well.

"So, you're like...in this, huh?"

"Yeah, I am."

"Well, Mama is over the moon about all of this."

"So is Ian's mom, she's already planning to throw us this huge reception party."

"You don't sound excited."

"I don't feel like she should be wasting all her money on a farce of a marriage, CiCi," Giselle said, feeling the guilt of lying to their parents rise up again.

"Look, you've already made a commitment to each other. Why not celebrate it?"

"I suppose you're right," Giselle relented.

"Of course, I'm right. Make sure you keep me posted. And I'll be looking for my invitation in the mail."

"No doubt," Giselle said.

They talked for several more minutes before Giselle got off of the phone and went back into the bedroom.

Her breath stalled when the en suite door opened and Ian walked out, dripping wet from having just taken a shower.

His eyes locked with hers and darkened when he noticed the way she licked her lips.

"Looks like Mrs. Noble is ready for another round," he said, dropping the towel.

He ambled over to her, lifted her up and tossed her on to the bed.

As he kissed his way up between her legs, while undoing her robe, she thought to herself that being Mrs. Ian Noble would definitely have some amazing perks.

Chapter Twenty-Two

The next day, Ian and Giselle were elbow deep in moving boxes. They were packing up her things; some would go to Ian's house, while the rest would go into storage.

"We'll probably have to make a few trips," Ian said, taping up another box.

"We can do it later this week," she said. "I'm actually scheduled to teach an aerial yoga class early tomorrow evening. And I'm paid up until the end of the month for my rent."

Though she'd completely flipped her world upside down by agreeing to stay married to Ian, Giselle wanted to keep most of her life as normal as possible. And that included continuing on with the things she loved to do. She had no plans on changing herself just because she was Mrs. Ian Noble. She'd done that once when she was too young and too naïve to understand what she was doing. She wasn't going to do it again.

But the amazing thing about Ian was that he had no desire to change her. They were completely open and honest with one another and accepted each other, with no judgement. Though, to her, Ian had probably been misjudged more than he deserved.

"Do you have a spare key?" Ian asked. "I can handle it."

"Are you sure?" she asked.

"Yeah, I'll get Isaiah to help, we'll be done in no time."

Giselle went to get the spare key and gave it to Ian. He hooked it to his key ring and then looked around.

"What do you want me to pack for the house next?" he asked.

"The picture frames off of the mantel."

Ian went over and began wrapping the photos, while Giselle headed for the kitchen, to pack up more dishes for storage. She stopped and looked at her silk hammock. She wondered if there was somewhere at Ian's house that he'd be okay with her installing it so she could continue practicing and choreographing her routines.

Deciding not to dwell on it for the time being, she continued on to the kitchen.

They worked quietly for a while, music from Giselle's phone filling the apartment, until she heard Ian call her name.

"Hey, Giselle?"

She looked up when she caught the strange lilt in his voice.

"How long has it been?"

She stared at him in confusion. "How long has what been?"

He held up a frame and she felt the air whoosh out of her lungs.

"How long has it been since you had cancer?"

She shut her eyes for a moment and swallowed hard. She knew she'd have to tell him eventually, he'd already seen the tattoo.

"I guess it's time for that story."

Ian sat down on the bar stool, while Giselle leaned over the island, gazing down at the picture she'd taken from him. While he was packing the photos like she'd instructed, he'd come across a picture of what was obviously Giselle as a teenager. What was shocking about the photo was seeing Giselle in a hospital bed, completely bald, with tubes hooked up to her. There was another young woman in the picture, and Ian figured it must be her sister.

Giselle's eyes were sunken in and dark and she looked so frail. But what stood out was she was still smiling.

"Acute lymphocytic leukemia," Giselle said, quietly. "I was diagnosed when I was sixteen."

"Jesus, Gi..." he whispered.

"It was absolute hell. Finding out that you have cancer at one of the most crucial times of your young adult life," she shook her head. "I'd barely gotten my license. I missed my prom."

He'd never gone to a prom either, but that was because he and his sibling had graduated high school early. He figured now was not the time to bring that up, so instead he said, "I can't even begin to imagine what you went through." He looked at the picture and gave her a gentle smile. "You seemed to be in good spirits on the day this picture was taken."

"That's because that was the day my sister saved my life."

"Your sister?"

Giselle nodded, her eyes growing misty. "She, uh...she got tested to see if she was a bone marrow match."

"And she was?" Ian guessed. "That's what the tattoo on your shoulder represents."

"Yeah, she has the same tattoo on the opposite shoulder."

They were silent for a few minutes before Ian asked the question that had been on his mind since he'd first discovered the picture. "Are you still..."

"Sick?" Giselle shook her head. "I've been in remission for over ten years now."

"That's good," he said.

"I go to the doctor every year for a checkup. I had my last appointment about eight months ago."

Her voice was shaky and he noticed a single tear fall down her cheek. She swiped it away. "I hope you're not upset with me."

Ian's eyes bucked wide. "Why would I be upset?"

"You've always been upfront with me about your life, and I've been keeping this from you. I should have told you about this before."

Ian was alarmed by the sob Giselle released and he was off the stool in a flash.

"Of course, I'm not upset," he said pulling her into his arms. "Baby, this was your story to tell, when you were ready, not a minute sooner. If anything, I'm sorry for making you relive a difficult time in your life."

He felt her wrap her arms around his waist and he held her tight as her small trembles subsided.

"Are you okay?" he asked.

She nodded. "I always get emotional talking about that time."

"Again, I'm sorry about that."

"Don't be," she said, shaking her head.

"Why don't we quit for the day?" he suggested. "We can take these boxes to my car and head home. I'll cook."

"That sounds good."

She pulled out of his embrace and he watched as she headed back to the living room. Giselle always had a 'live life to the fullest' vibe about her, and Ian understood the reason why now more than ever.

"Now reach up, grab your hammock and gently pull yourself up to a standing position...return to the front of your yoga mat, palms together at your heart center." Giselle inhaled deeply, encouraging her class to do so as well.

"Namaste," she said after several more relaxing breaths, signaling the end of class. She stayed for a few minutes longer, helping some of the students who stuck around for pointers and then left the classroom.

"Giselle!"

She turned when she saw Dana and Tessa coming toward her.

"Hey," she said to the sisters. "You two getting out of hot yoga?"

"Yes," Dana said, rolling her eyes at her older sister. "But next week, we'll be taking *your* class. I'd much rather hang upside down for an hour rather than burn up for ninety minutes."

"It's not that bad," Tessa said, bumping Dana's arm with her own. "And you know you love it. But I'm down to try your class, Giselle. It looks like it's actually a lot of fun."

"It's quite relaxing," Giselle said. "I think you'll enjoy it."

"Hey!" Dana said. "Tessa and I are going out to eat after we get cleaned up. You should join us."

Giselle adjusted the strap on her gym bag. "Oh...I don't know. Ian's at my place getting my stuff packed and moved. I should probably go over and help."

Tessa waved her hand. "Isaiah's over there helping him. Let those men do all of the manual labor."

After everything that had gone on over the last few days, coming in to teach her yoga class had helped tremendously, but she figured a little extra down time couldn't hurt.

"Just let me shoot Ian a quick text."

She pulled out her phone and found his name in her phone.

Just got out of yoga class. Ran into Tessa & Dana. They invited me out to dinner.

As she, Tessa and Dana headed to the locker room to wait for available shower stalls, Ian responded.

Ian: Go. We're loading up the last box and heading home. I'll see you later tonight.

Giselle placed her phone in her bag.

It looked like it was going to be a girl's night out.

Chapter Twenty-Three

"To Giselle Noble!" Dana said, as they toasted their margaritas.

"Wow," Giselle said. "That's the first time I've heard someone say that."

"It has a nice ring to it," Tessa said, smiling.

"So, how does it feel to be married to Ian Noble?" Dana asked.

Giselle shrugged and swirled the straw in her glass around. "I mean everything happened so fast. We didn't really think about it."

"Ugh, but that's just it," Tessa said, slamming her glass down. "The two of you didn't think, you just went for it. Isaiah used to be spontaneous like that."

Giselle's eyes grew wide at her friend's outburst.

"Don't mind her," Dana said. "She's just all antsy because it's been over a year and Isaiah still hasn't proposed."

"Oh," Giselle said. "I wouldn't worry about that, Tessa. Everyone knows how crazy Isaiah is about you. He's going to propose."

She remembered Ian briefly mentioning that Isaiah

planned on proposing soon. She glanced over to Dana and they shared a knowing look.

"I *know* he's going to propose," Tessa said. "But knowing him, he's probably trying to figure out some huge elaborate way to propose."

"And what's wrong with that?" Dana said. "Quit overthinking, like you always do, and let that man do things how he's going to do them."

"You're right," Tessa said with a moue of resignation. "I'm just ready to be married to Isaiah. You know I'm just as crazy about him. And we've been living together for a year now."

"And he's been busy, honey. He's been transitioning into taking over Noble Naturals, on top of finding time to keep producing music on the side *and* somehow managing to direct another short film. Your man is making waves."

Giselle watched as Tessa relaxed at her younger sister's words.

They settled in, continued chatting and drinking.

They were eating their food and on their second margarita when Giselle noticed Dana grow tense.

"Shit," Dana whispered, a scowl crossing her face.

Tessa looked up and sighed. "Dana, don't do anything stupid."

"I'm not going to do anything stupid," Dana said, rolling her eyes.

Giselle turned to see what the other two women were looking at and saw the tall, gorgeous man walking toward their table.

"Good evening ladies."

"Hi, Aiden," both Tessa and Giselle said. Dana remained silent and avoided his gaze.

Aiden looked down at Giselle and smiled. "I hear congratulations are in order."

"Thank you," Giselle said, returning his smile.

"And I hear you ladies have a lot to celebrate too," Aiden said, addressing Tessa since Dana seemed to be looking everywhere but at Aiden. "I'm sure you're excited about the opening of your second location in Carson City."

"We are. Thanks, Aiden," Tessa said, giving him a sympathetic smile.

Aiden looked at Dana and Giselle noticed a hint of resentment and pain in his eyes. He cleared his throat and then said, "I won't take up any more your time. I'll see you around."

Once he was gone, Tessa turned to Dana, glaring at her with censure.

"Did you have to be so damn rude?"

"He didn't speak to *me*," Dana snapped back.

"He addressed the whole table, and he was looking directly at you when he said good evening. *You* didn't speak back."

When Dana refused to speak, Giselle asked, "What's going on?"

Tessa turned to Giselle. "They fooled around for about six months. But then Aiden started getting more serious and Dana ended things." She glanced at her sister. "I *still* think that was a huge mistake by the way."

"We had an arrangement. *He* was the one who ended things."

"You fought and you fucked," Tessa argued. "And he ended things with you because every time he tried to move the relationship forward, you did something to push him away."

"Look, can we not talk about this anymore, it's putting a damper on the mood and we're supposed to be celebrating Giselle."

Tessa smiled at Giselle. "Dana's right. Sorry Giselle."

"Don't be," Giselle said.

They continued eating, drinking and the mood soon perked up again.

Her phone vibrated and she pulled it out of her pocket.

Ian: Having fun?

Yes, we're just finishing up. I should be headed home soon.

She was already referring to his house as home.

Ian: Would it be weird for me to say I missed my wife and I can't wait for you to get here?

Giselle smiled at his text. Suddenly she realized she was extremely eager to see him as well.

Not at all.

Ian: Then hurry up and get that fine ass home to your husband.

She threw enough cash to cover her part of the meal and stood.

"Thanks for inviting me out to eat with you. But I'm about to head home."

"Me too," Tessa said quickly, putting her phone down.

"Oh I see. Judging from the goofy ass grins on both of your faces, your men must have sent you texts."

"The way Aiden keeps looking at you across the restaurant, I don't think it would be hard to convince him to go home with you," Tessa said, wiggling her eyes.

"He should be so lucky."

"All right," Tessa said in a warning tone. "You keep messing around with that man's emotions, pretty soon he's going to stop waiting around for you."

Giselle said good-bye and then went to her car.

She got to the house and unlocked the door with the key he'd given her earlier that day.

"Ian?" she called out.

She heard footsteps overhead and looked up when he appeared at the top of the stairs. They stared at each other for several moments before Giselle headed for the stairs. The slight buzz humming through her body aroused her even more as she climbed the stairs one by one.

Ian didn't say a word; he just watched her, his eyes smoldering.

When she reached the top stair, he looked down at her and licked his lips.

"How did the moving go?" she asked.

He took her hand and led her to one of the spare rooms.

"Open the door," he said.

Giselle grabbed the handle, pushed the door open and gasped. She turned and looked at Ian, who was standing behind her with a grin. She walked further into the room and raised her hand to her silk hammock hanging from the ceiling.

"You'll have to inspect it, make sure it's installed correctly, but I think it's up there right."

"It looks...perfect." She gave it a tug and it felt good and sturdy. "It feels perfect."

"You know," Ian said, finally entering the room. "You never did give me that private show."

"Hmmm," she said, looking at him. She walked back over to him, ran her hands up his chest then gave him a shove, forcing him to fall into the chair in the room. Then she pulled her phone out, went into one of her playlists and turned on a slow song. She kicked her shoes off as the first few bars of the song played and then turned to face him again.

"Are you ready for Gypsy?" she teased in a seductive purr.

She slowly glided toward him, moving her hips to the beat. She stopped in front of him, pushed her pants down, revealing her lace boy shorts. She spun on the balls of feet, putting her ass in his face. She felt his hands glide up her the back of her thighs, before she moved out of his grasp, strutting toward the silks. She pulled her shirt over her head and tossed it off to the side.

She was now down to her lacy lingerie, as she circled the

hammock several times, moving her body sensuously to the beat. Finally, she reached up, grabbed the silks with both hands and wrapped them loosely around her wrists. She gripped them tightly as she flipped her body backwards. She hung upside down, her feet in the air before bending her legs. She brought her body upright, and did several other tricks, twisting and contorting her body several ways, before she stretched the hammock out around her, before doing a slow body roll.

She could feel Ian's burning gaze on her, as she sat up, and hooked the silks around both feet and did a full split as the song ended.

Ian stood and moved toward her.

"Did you enjoy the show?" she asked, slightly out of breath.

"Thoroughly."

She moved to undo her legs, but Ian stopped her. He slowly ran his hand over both legs which were spread open.

"When I was at your place finishing up with the packing, I came across your...treasure trove."

Her eyes rounded like saucers. Why hadn't she thought to pack that herself?

Her train of thought became mush, when he pulled his hand out of his pocket and had her small bullet hooked around his finger.

Her hands gripped the silks tighter as he stepped into her space.

He looked at the tiny vibrator and said, "You have quite the collection, Gi. But I was particularly fascinated by this one." He pushed the button and the buzzing sound filled the air along with her labored breathing. "Is this the one you used that night I went home after our date? Or did you use one of the bigger ones?"

Her head fell back as he pressed his finger against her center, stroking her above the fabric of her panties causing her to moan loudly.

"Which one did you use while you thought of me?" he asked. "Was it this one?"

"Yes," she breathed.

"Let's see what this thing can do," he said, pushing her panties to the side. He brushed the bullet against her clit and Giselle moaned again.

"Shit...Ian."

She watched him as he dipped his finger inside of her. The vibrations, along with Ian's steady pumping drove her insane. She'd used her little toy on herself countless times, but with Ian controlling it, the intensity was off the charts.

Her legs grew limp as she came. She pulled her legs out of the split and leaned back in the hammock, feeling spent. Ian's hands trailed up her thighs, pulled her panties off and suddenly his face was buried between her legs.

Giselle swore again as Ian sucked her clit between his lips. She nearly came again from that one move. He continued to feast on her, making love to her with his mouth as if she were his last meal.

Soon another orgasm washed over her. She was too spent to move, so Ian scooped her up out of the hammock and carried her to the bed.

After he undressed, he climbed onto the bed. She pushed him on his back, straddled his lap and then sank down on his hardness.

She started off slow, rolling her body the same way she had when she was in the hammock, performing for him. But then she sped up and rode him hard, driving him up the wall like he'd done to her in her hammock. When his orgasm was on the brink, he gripped her hips and thrust upward until they both shattered.

She collapsed on his chest and he wrapped his arms around her, kissing her temple before they both drifted off to sleep.

Chapter Twenty-Four

Ian smiled at Giselle as he adjusted the beekeeper veil on her head.

"I must look ridiculous," she murmured.

He chuckled, unzipped the veil and lifted it to give her a quick kiss on the lips. She looked ridiculously adorable, he thought.

"You're fine, Gi. This isn't exactly about making a fashion statement. Safety first," he said as he zipped the veil back. "Are you ready?"

"I guess," she said.

He placed his own veil on and stepped back to inspect Giselle in the beekeeping suit.

Everything looked good, so he grabbed the smoker off of the table and handed to Giselle before picking up the rest of the supplies they needed.

"Let's go."

They made their way out to the beehive.

"I added the escape to the super a few days ago, so the honey should be ready."

"Ian, you realize I have no clue what you're talking about, right?"

"Oh...yeah," he said, as they stopped in front of the hive. He sat the items he'd been carrying down and pointed at the top boxes. "Each of these is called a honey super, it's where the bees store their honey. The escape is a type of board that's added so that the bees can go down into this lower box, which is called the brood, giving us the opportunity to take out the frames in the supers that have the capped honey on them."

Giselle nodded seeming to follow along.

"I brought out some clean frames to replace the ones we pull out. First things first, I need you to use the smoker around the hive, to calm the bees down. Like I showed you back at the green house."

Giselle began to use the smoker.

"Good," Ian said as he removed the top super and opened up the hive. He took the frames out and handed them to Giselle. "Put these in the tub I brought out."

"Wow, these are heavier than they look," she said as she put them in the uncapping tub.

Ian refilled the super with fresh frames. "That means we'll have a good harvest this season."

He removed the bee escape, added a bit more smoke and then replaced the top super.

"We'll come back out in a few weeks to see if there's more capped honey to extract. Don't forget the smoker," he said as he lifted the tub and they made their trek back to the greenhouse.

He sat the tub on one of the worktables and after Giselle closed the door behind them, removed his veil.

"I prefer extracting the honey in here simply because once the honey is out of the hive, it attracts the bees more, along with other insects."

"I'm not complaining about avoiding bugs," Giselle said.

When Ian had gotten up earlier, he told Giselle he was going out to the beehive and invited her along. He was surprised when she, rather enthusiastically, agreed.

After they removed their outfits and hung them back up, they went back to the table. Ian pulled a frame out.

"We're going to use this heated knife to cut the capped honey out of the frame. I use foundationless frames."

"What does that mean?" she asked, watching as he cut the honey out of the frame.

"Simply that there's no foundation on which the bees build the honeycombs."

He cut a small piece of the honeycomb off and held it up to her mouth. "Here, taste it."

"I can eat it, just like this?" she asked.

"Of course you can. You won't taste anything better than fresh honey."

She opened her mouth, and he fed it to her. She chewed for a few seconds before her eyes lit up.

"That's so good."

"Told you," he said, before he got back to work cutting the rest of the capped honey from the other frames and putting them into a clean bucket.

"Now we have to crush the honey, before we put it in the straining system." He handed her a wire masher. "I know you're strong as shit with all that aerial silk work you do. Start crushing woman."

Giselle snatched the masher from him and moved to stand in front of him. She carefully moved the utensil up and down slowly. Ian chuckled, and wrapped his arms around her, folding his hands over hers.

"Come on, girl. You can do better than that. Get up in there."

"It's so sticky!" she giggled.

"Duh, it's honey. Of course, it's sticky. You know that very intimately," he said in her ear, reminding her of their tryst on the kitchen island when he'd drizzled honey all over her body.

He helped her mash up the honeycomb until everything was crushed.

"That's how you do it," he said, stepping back.

"Now what?" Giselle asked.

"Now," he said, picking up the bucket. "We pour it in here and let nature and gravity take over. We'll come back out tomorrow and fill up those bottle from the tap."

"So, we're done for now?"

"Yep."

They left the greenhouse, hopped into the utility vehicle and headed for the house.

"Thank you for showing me that," Giselle said. "It was interesting and fun."

"You're welcome. Now that I've got you here, I may put you to work," he teased.

"I'll be glad to help."

She'd helped out in more ways than he would have imagined. And he found himself growing more and more thankful for that.

"Hey, Gi!" Ian called out as he walked back into the house, tearing open a large envelope. "It's here."

"The show's contract?" she asked, rushing down the stairs.

He nodded when she got to his side. He pulled the large stack of papers out. "They sent it over to Michelle first so she and my lawyer could look it over and see if there were any changes that needed to be made. They also emailed a digital copy of the contract."

A large smile spread across his face as he began to read it. "At home with Ian..." he said quietly. "It's really happening."

Giselle smiled as well before she grabbed a pen. "Only one thing left to do," she said, handing him the pen.

They sat down on the sofa and Ian set the contract down on the table before he flipped to the page to sign. He leaned over to sign but froze, the pen hovering just above the paper.

"Ian?" Giselle said, touching his shoulder. "Ian, what's wrong?"

He looked at Giselle, her eyes full of concern and it touched him.

He reached into the envelope and pulled out another set of papers.

"This contract is yours," he said. "Of course since you agreed to occasionally appear on the show with me, as my wife, you have to sign one to."

"Oh, is that all?" she asked with a smile. She grabbed the pen from Ian's hand, went to the last page in her set of documents and, without hesitation, went to sign.

"Wait," Ian said, reaching out to grab her hand to stop her.

She looked up at him, confused.

"*What* is the matter, Ian?"

"Gi, are you *absolutely* sure about this? This is kind of your last chance to back out. Once you sign that contract, you're basically stuck with me. Even if we dissolve the marriage, you'll still be contractually obligated to do the number of shows in this contract. And even though we're in the pilot season, the contract is for five years if we get renewed."

"Ian, we've discussed this multiple times," Giselle said. "I'm pretty sure that night when we were drunk, me saying that I'd marry you in a heartbeat, is part of the reason we ended up saying 'I Do' through a limo sunroof at a drive-thru chapel. I'm just as much to blame for this situation as you are. This is your dream, and if we have to stay married for a while, then I'm game. So we're in this together. Besides, you can't beat free room and board, great food and fantastic sex."

"Fantastic, huh?" Ian repeated with a grin.

"Don't sit there and act like you don't know what you're working with, Ian Noble."

She turned her attention back to the papers and before he could stop her again, she scrolled her signature across the line.

"Your turn," she said, handing him the pen again.

He took the pen, looked at the paper and then signed it.

"Congratulations, Ian," Giselle said, her eyes twinkling with a humbling pride. "You officially have your own television show!"

Chapter Twenty-Five

"Gi...Giselle." Ian shook Giselle's sleeping body. "Baby, wake up."

Ian had quickly learned that his new wife wasn't exactly a morning person. Giselle grumbled a few expletives in her sleep and pulled the blanket up over her head.

Ian tugged the blanket off and smacked her ass. "Come on, it's back to work today."

He was in the shower, when he heard the door open. He turned as Giselle stepped inside.

She grinned at him and then he watched as she dropped to her knees and took him into her mouth.

"Gi," he gritted through his teeth. "Fuck, Giselle."

His back hit the wall and he looked down, watching as her head bobbed back and forth. She took him in deeply and then pulled back, letting her tongue ring slide slowly along his manhood until she reached the tip. His knees buckled when he felt that cool metal ball swirl sensuously around the head before she went back to greedily sucking and stroking him at the same time. He dug his hands into her hair and he worked his hips.

"Giselle, baby, I'm about to..." He tried to pull away when

he felt his orgasm quickly approaching, but she seemed to take even more of him into her mouth.

He exploded and she didn't stop until she had taken every last drop from him.

Finally, she stood.

"Good morning," she said, before pressing her lips to his chest.

He lifted her up, pressed her against the wall and slid inside of her.

"More like great morning," he growled.

Two hours later, Giselle came into the kitchen dressed and ready for work as Ian filled their travel mugs with coffee.

"We're late now, thanks to you," he murmured with a grin.

Giselle had joined him in the shower and the memory of the things she'd done to his dick with her mouth and that tongue ring...

"You don't look like you're complaining," Giselle said, taking one of the mugs from his hand.

"Oh, I'm not. I was simply stating a fact." He put the top on his mug and took a sip. "Do you want to ride together or separate?"

"Separate," Giselle said. "I have to leave work on time today. I've got rehearsal tonight at Joie de Burlesque."

"Oh, I got a text from my mom earlier. She invited us to dinner tomorrow night. She said she wanted to discuss more plans for this reception party."

"Sounds good."

"She's not bombarding you with all of that, is she?"

"Of course not," Giselle said. "Your mother is sweet."

Ian nodded as he grabbed his keys off of the counter.

They both drove to Noble Naturals and when they entered the building, they headed straight for the elevator.

Once they arrived on their floor, they grabbed their lab

coats and went into the lab where they were greeted with a loud round of applause.

Their co-workers cheered and whistled, shouting their congratulations.

"Give your bride a kiss," one of the older workers yelled.

Ian and Giselle looked at each other and then attempted to politely decline by shaking their heads, but their co-workers wouldn't take no for an answer. Soon they were chanting, "Kiss her...kiss her...kiss her."

Ian held up his hands to calm them down, and then turned to Giselle. She laughed as he pulled her into his arms, spun her slightly and then dipped her before planting a big kiss on her lips, which garnered loud catcalling and more whistling.

Ian sat her back up and the crowd surrounded them with hugs and handshakes. As Ian and Giselle accepted all of the well wishes, he took notice of one employee standing off in a corner glaring in their direction, obviously not enthusiastic like the rest of their co-workers.

Walsh.

"Okay," Giselle said over the loud hum in the lab. "We appreciate you all, but it's time to get to work."

Everyone dispersed and Giselle grabbed Ian's arm.

"I had an idea on the drive in to work."

"What's up?" he asked, as they walked in to her office and he shut the door.

"I want to create a new line with honey as one of the components."

"Honey?" Ian repeated.

"Yeah," Giselle said, nodding her head. "I was thinking about how I helped you with the hive last week. And honey is good for the body, inside and out, head to toe. We can find another ingredient to mix with it."

"African black soap," Ian said.

"That's a great idea!"

"I like the idea too. But Gi, we'd have to start from scratch and we already have most of the lines done. It's going to be a lot of work, tweaking everything from the tester feedback on top of creating a whole new line."

"I know," she said. "But it's not like it's just the two of us. We have a whole team out there."

"You really want to do this, huh?"

"Yes."

Ian sighed and shoved his hands in his pockets. "You're the boss," he said. "I'll help as much as I can, until production for the show starts."

"Thank you!" she said, kissing his lips.

"Mrs. Noble, behave yourself," he teased with a wink before he opened the door and they went to their lab tables to start working.

The day went by surprisingly fast and at quitting time, Giselle said goodbye to Ian and headed to Joie de Burlesque.

The rehearsal went well and afterward, she headed to the bar where the bartender had a bottle of water waiting for her.

She dabbed the light sheen of sweat from her forehead before she opened the bottle and took a long gulp.

"Looks like it's gonna be another great performance," Frank said, stopping in front of her.

"I'm glad you think so," Giselle said with a smile. She looked at her watch. "I gotta go, Frank."

"Gotta get home to that new husband of yours?" he said with a wink.

"Yeah," she said, laughing as she picked up her bag. "I'll see you this weekend."

It was dark by the time she left and headed for her car.

"Giselle!"

She jumped and turned quickly. Then her eyebrows bunched together in confusion.

"Thomas?" She looked around and then back at him. "What are you doing here?"

"How could you do something so *stupid*?" She caught the slur in his voice and the sway in his walk, along with his disheveled clothes. "I warned you about him. But did you listen? No!"

Giselle took a step back and her body bumped her car.

"And I told you, what I do and whom I do it with is none of your concern."

"I asked you out all of the time. Gave you gifts–"

"Which I always returned. You knew my stance with you."

"'I don't date co-workers'. That's what you said, over and over whenever I asked you out. But Noble is here for a few months and you end up marrying him! You're full of shit, Giselle."

"And you're drunk as hell. Thomas, you need to leave."

Before she could move around him, Thomas slammed his hands on the hood of her car near her head. She turned away from him, his liquor-filled breath in her face.

"Thomas," she said through clenched teeth, growing angrier by the second. "You need to move...*now*!"

"You must have some magic pussy to get Ian Noble to settle down so fucking fast. As much work as I put in perusing you, I think you owe me a sample as well," he taunted, reaching for her thigh.

Giselle jerked her leg away from Thomas' hand before reaching up to slap him across the face.

"Don't fucking touch me," she yelled, before kicking him in the groin. When he doubled over, she tried to run, but he reached out, grabbed her arm and threw her against the car again. Blinding pain filled her face as Thomas backhanded her.

"So you like it rough. I always figured you did," he said, as he wrapped his hand around her neck.

Giselle continued fighting as hard as she could against him; kicking, scratching, whatever she needed to do. She was preparing to ram the heel of her palm up his nose when Thomas' crazed eyes were suddenly filled with shock as he was hauled away from Giselle by Ian.

The relief that flooded her body hit her in waves.

"Don't you ever put another fucking finger on my wife again," Ian roared as he threw Thomas to the ground and proceeded to throw punch after punch to the man's face and body.

The door to the club burst open and several men rushed out. They grabbed Ian and pull him off of Thomas.

Frank came out with a baseball bat in hand.

"I'm pressing charges," Thomas yelled out.

"Yeah, I'd like to see you try," Frank yelled back. He pointed the baseball bat at Thomas. "Get the fuck outta here before I finish what Ian started."

Thomas stumbled off to his car and peeled out of the parking lot, tires screeching.

Ian went to Giselle and pulled her into his arms and she wrapped her arms around his waist, still thankful that he was there.

"You good, GiGi?" Frank asked.

"I'm good," she said, though her body was still trembling. It was more from anger than fear.

"We saw that creep on camera and when he started getting rough with you, me and the boys decided to come out and send him on his way. Noble, you came out of nowhere."

"I'm just glad I got here when I did," Ian said. It was obvious he was still mad as hell the way his body emanated with rage. "Are you sure you're okay?" he asked.

"Thanks to you," Giselle said.

"You seemed to be holding your own pretty well," he said, brushing a loose strand of hair out of her face. He turned to Frank. "I'm going to take her home in my car. We'll pick hers up tomorrow."

Frank nodded his head. "We'll keep a good eye on it for you."

Ian picked up her bag and kept her close to his side as they walked to his car.

The ride home was filled with a thick silence.

When they arrived at home, Ian sat her bag down by the door and turned to Giselle. He reached out and cupped her face and she winced. Ian pushed her hair out of the way and saw the large purple bruise on her cheek and neck.

"I'm gonna kill that motherfucker."

"Ian, don't," she said, grabbing his arm. "You already beat the shit out of him. This...this will heal."

He balled his fists, clearly wanting to hit something again. He blew out a long breath. They went into the kitchen and he grabbed an ice pack out of the fridge and gingerly covered her face. Then he went and grabbed some aspirin and a bottle of water.

As she took the pills, Ian said, "I decided to leave work and come by the club to watch you practice. But I got caught in traffic on the way to Carson City. If I'd gotten there sooner–"

"You got there at just the right time. Nothing happened. Nothing was *going* to happen. I wasn't going to let Thomas do anything to me."

"You're one hell of a fighter."

"My daddy taught me well," she said, smiling and then realizing even that hurt.

"I can't wait to meet him," Ian said.

"Yeah, I can't wait for you to meet him either."

Soon she began to feel sleepy. "What did you give me?"

"A sleep aid aspirin," he said. "Come on, you should rest."

She was about to stand when he reached down and picked her up in his arms. He carried her upstairs, undressed her and then himself and slid into the bed.

"Are your knuckles okay?" she asked, drowsily.

She felt him kiss the back of her head and then say, "Don't you worry about me."

She felt safe in the warmth of his arms and as she drifted off to sleep, she sent up a silent prayer of thanks.

She knew she could handle herself against Thomas, but there was something comforting in knowing she didn't have to because of Ian.

Chapter Twenty-Six

Isaiah sat back in his office chair, clearly trying to rein in his temper.

"He won't step a goddamned foot in this building again," he said to Ian, who was furiously pacing the floor, referring to Thomas.

Ian swung around to face his brother. "He'd better not. I don't even want him breathing the same fucking air as Giselle. If I ever see that bastard again, I'm going to do what I should have done last night."

"We're lucky he didn't go through with trying to pressing charges."

"*He's* lucky his ass didn't end up in a body bag. And fuck Walsh! Even if he tried to press charges, there's video proof at the club showing him..." Ian slammed his fists on Isaiah's desk. "He put his hands on my wife, Isaiah!"

"I know..." Isaiah said. "How is Giselle?"

Ian shook his head. "Her face is still swollen and her back is still bothering her." He squeezed his eyes shut, against the memory of the bruising he'd found on her back when he'd undressed her the night before. "But other than that, she seems to be doing well. We went down to the police station this morning and she pressed charges against Walsh and filed for a restraining order."

"That's good, tell her to take all the time she needs."

Ian nodded and headed for the door.

He didn't bother staying at work. There's no way he'd be able to focus. So he went home, to Giselle.

She was asleep on the couch when he got home.

Seeing Walsh manhandle her the way he did the night before had set off a rage in him unlike anything he'd ever experienced before. He was glad that Giselle had held her own against him, but his mind still ran rampant about what would have happened if he hadn't decided to go and see her at the club. Even though she was clearly well versed in self-defense, she was still at a disadvantage against a man who was bigger than her, as well as drunk.

She shifted on the couch and her eyes slid open. When she saw him, sitting on the coffee table in front of her, she smiled and sat up.

"Hey," she said. "What are you doing home so early?"

"I decided not to stay at work," he replied. "How's your face feeling?"

The swelling had gone down a little, but the bruising was still prominent.

"Still hurts like a bitch. What did Isaiah say when you told him about last night?"

"He's taking care of everything. Don't worry about it."

"I'm not worried," Giselle said. "I just wanted to know."

"Walsh has been terminated, effective immediately."

"Good," Giselle said, pulling the blanket tight around her shoulders.

"Are you okay?" he asked.

"I'm fine, Ian. I'm just cold."

He sat down next to her and wrapped his arms around her, helping to warm her.

"I'll need to figure out what I'm going to wear tonight for dinner at your mother's."

"We don't have to do that, Gi. After last night–"

"I want things to be as normal as possible," she said. "And that means going to your mother's for dinner."

"What about–"

"My face?" she finished what he hesitated to say. She smiled. "It's nothing a little cover up won't fix."

"Fine," he said. "I'll let her know dinner is still on."

"Oh Giselle, honey. How are you?" Irene asked, pulling her into a tight hug when she and Ian entered her home later that evening.

"I'm doing just fine," Giselle said. "I'd never let some a–uh *jerk* mess with me."

"Ata girl," she said, smiling. "Come to the dining room. I wanted to discuss your reception party. I think I've got a date narrowed down."

Giselle looked over her shoulder at Ian, who was behind her and his mother.

"Now," Irene continued. "Tessa's grand opening for the second bakery is in a couple of months and I'm helping her mother plan the party for that as well. So how does a month after that sound? Giselle, I spoke to your parents and they said that was the next time they were free to take off from work."

"You spoke to my parents?" Giselle asked, surprise.

"Oh yes, weeks ago. Your parents are wonderful people. Your mother and I chatted for hours. Have you let them know about...what happened?"

Giselle looked down and nodded. "This morning."

"So, you want to do the reception three months from now?" Ian asked, changing the subject. He squeezed Giselle's thigh under the table and she looked up at him and smiled. He understood that she wanted to move past the incident with Thomas.

"That will give us time to plan, send out invitations and get their RSVPs back; all that good stuff," Irene said.

"I guess that's fine with me, what do you think, Gi?"

"Sounds good to me too."

"Good!" Irene said, clapping her hands. "Oh, I can't wait!"

"Me neither," Giselle said with a smile.

They sat down for dinner and she and Irene were chatty through the meal. She noticed how Ian was oddly quiet during the entire evening and on the drive home.

When they reached the bedroom, she turned to him, pressing her body to his.

"I enjoyed dinner, but I'm glad to be home."

She pressed her lips to his and he gave her hips a gentle squeeze before pulling away.

"You must be exhausted. Let's get you into bed."

"I'm not tired," she said, reaching for his belt buckle as she licked her lips. "After sleeping most of the day, I'm actually quite full of energy."

Ian gave her a weary smile and gently moved her hands away.

"I'm pretty worn out, sweetheart. I think I'm ready to turn in for the night."

He kissed her forehead again and turned to head for the bathroom, leaving her standing in the middle of the bedroom.

Giselle woke up in the middle of the night and noticed Ian's side of the bed was empty.

Again.

It had been two weeks since the incident with Thomas and something was off with Ian.

On one hand, he was more attentive and caring than he'd ever been, but on the other hand, he'd been the perfect gentleman when it came to them being intimate together.

Too damn perfect, and she was hornier than she could ever remember.

Her ears perked up at the sound of a guitar softly playing somewhere close by. She pushed the covers off of her and got out of the bed. She followed the music and found herself climbing the stairs to the rooftop patio.

It was honestly one of Giselle's favorite places of the house. Ian had it set up with comfortable outdoor furniture and on clear nights, like tonight, it felt like you could almost reach up and touch the stars.

Ian's back was facing her, but she could see his fingers expertly dancing across the strings of an acoustic guitar. She walked around to the front of the couch and noticed Ian's eyes were closed.

He must have sensed her presence because his eyes opened and his lip quirked up at the sight of her. He nodded his head to the seat next to him and she sat down, tucking her feet underneath her, and settled in to listen to Ian play.

She rested her head on the back of the couch, gazing up at the stars in the sky and after listening to a few bars, Giselle realized she recognized the song he was playing. She closed her eyes and began to sing along to Ian's playing of the popular old love song.

Once the song ended, she opened her eyes again and found Ian staring at her in a peculiar way.

"I shouldn't be surprised that you sing so beautifully," he said quietly, as his lips tilted up into a grin.

She waved her hand, tossing his compliment off. "I don't know how I forgot you played the guitar."

"One of the many talents of the Noble Quads," he murmured.

Giselle remembered when Isaiah and Isabella had played their instruments at their father's funeral the previous year. How they'd gotten through that without breaking down was beyond Giselle. She'd been a mess at the funeral and Isaac Noble wasn't even her father.

She reached out and gently ran her fingers across the shiny front of the instrument.

"I don't think I've ever seen a more beautiful guitar."

Ian looked down at it and grinned with pride.

"Yes, it's one of my favorites. That's why I keep it here."

"How many do you have?"

Ian sat back and thought. "I've got two here, two in storage in Vegas, which I need to bring home." Ian had decided to put his resignation in at the restaurant in Vegas, so he could spend more time in Sweet Rapids preparing for the cooking show. He also decided to offer the tenant renting his apartment in Vegas a longer contract with the option to buy. He no longer needed the place. "And I have two that stay in Isaiah's studio at his place is Lake Tahoe."

"I bet that place is beautiful."

"It is. You'll love it when we go for the party they're having after the grand opening." He sat his guitar down and then asked, "What are you doing up? I didn't wake you with my playing, did I?"

"No," Giselle said, smiling. "As odd as it may sound, I actually find myself having a hard time sleeping when you're not in the bed with me. But I guess that's what happens when you've been married for a month now. Did you realize today's the day?"

Ian nodded. "Yeah..."

Giselle crawled toward him and straddled his lap. "I know we're not the 'traditional couple'," she said, kissing his neck, feeling his erection growing and pressing against the juncture of her thighs. "But that doesn't mean we can't celebrate our anniversary accordingly, right?"

Ian sighed and moved his head to avoid her lips.

"Gi..." He gave her an uncomfortable smile.

Her hands dropped in disappointment. She knew that tone, had become all too familiar with it over the last two weeks. It was filled with rejection at her advances.

"Well, I guess the honeymoon is officially over," she said with frustration, as she got off of his lap.

"It's not that, Giselle."

"Then what the fuck is it?!" she yelled. There were no neighbors to be concerned about, but even if there were, she didn't give a damn at the moment. She glared at him. "Have I done something?"

"What?" Ian asked, shock evident on his face. "No, you haven't done anything."

"Then what is going on, Ian?" She became pissed at herself, when she noticed the slight shakiness in her voice and felt her eyes fill with tears. "You haven't touched me in two weeks."

Ian broke eye contact and looked away.

"Is there someone else?"

They'd never discussed exclusivity to one another, but Giselle had never felt the need to, not even before they'd run off and got married.

His wide eyes swung back to hers. "Of course there's no one else," he said, his brows bunching.

She blew out a huff of breath. "We never discussed exclusivity."

"I didn't think we had to. Gi, you should know me better than that by now."

"Then tell me what is going on with you?"

She sat down next to him, when he didn't say anything.

"We've always been open with each other," she said quietly. "But lately, it feels like...I don't know. It feels like you're pulling away from me. Are you...are you ready to end this marriage already?"

"No, Giselle."

"Then talk to me." She hated the pleading sound in her voice, but she couldn't seem to help herself.

Ian sat forward, pressing his elbow on his thighs.

"Every time I think about what Walsh tried to do to you..."

It finally all made sense. He was just trying to be careful with her. He probably assumed Giselle was traumatized from what happened.

"Ian," she said, quietly. "I'm fine. Nothing happened."

"He put his hands on you, Gi!" Ian said, the anger from that night was present on his face.

"So, because Thomas *tried* to touch me, now you won't?" Giselle asked, trying to keep her own anger in check. "Ian, if you've been hesitant because you think I feel like some victim, then you shouldn't, because I don't."

Ian blew out a frustrated breath. "I've just been trying to...I don't know, ease back in to things."

"I don't want you to 'ease back in to things'," she said, exasperated. She ran her hands through her hair. "I want...I want you to fuck me the way you did in that supply closet when we first met."

Chapter Twenty-Seven

Ian's eyes grew wide and his mouth dropped open at Giselle's comment.

She climbed onto his lap again.

"Ian, I know you want this as much as I do. I can feel it."

She rolled her body against his and she felt him grow even harder, and felt his fingers dig into her hips.

"Stop depriving us both," she whispered into his ear.

She sat back on his lap and locked eyes with him. The last bit of uncertainty washed away and was suddenly replaced with a look of unbridled passion. He dug his hands in her hair and yanked her to him, kissing her deeply.

She returned the kiss, excited to feel his hands and mouth on her again. She was surprised by how much she'd missed him over the last couple of weeks, despite going to work together every day and sleeping in the same bed every night.

He pushed her robe open and Giselle smiled when Ian cursed when he discovered she was naked. His head dipped low and his mouth locked onto her breast, tugging her nipple between his teeth.

She cried out, loving the sensations rocketing through her

body. There was something about being able to be uninhibited in the outdoors that amplified her arousal. She grabbed his shirt with both hands and ripped it open, not caring about the buttons that popped off in the process. They quickly worked at getting his pants off and then he laid her down on the couch.

He pushed his way inside of her and they both sighed at the connection. He pulled out slowly before entering her again. He took his time with her, kissing her gently, caressing her softly. There was something different this time.

It almost felt like...he was making love to her.

Out on the roof, beneath the billions of stars, Ian cherished her body in a way no man ever had before.

She could feel her orgasm building slowly, like a tsunami in the distance. And when it finally hit her, Ian came at the same time.

Both of their bodies were slick with perspiration and quivering from what they'd experienced.

He lifted his body slightly away from her and looked down at her. She was glad to see the shadows in his eyes gone.

"Happy anniversary, Gi."

She cupped his cheek and smiled. "It is now," she said, before pulling him back down to kiss her again.

Eventually, Ian carried her inside and downstairs to the bedroom, where he made love to her again.

And it was in the throes of passion, as Ian took her higher and higher that Giselle realized...

She just might be falling in love with her husband.

"Ian, come and check this out."

Ian looked up from his lab table and went over to Giselle's. She held her arm up.

"Feel."

He ran his fingers across her skin, which felt incredibly smooth.

"Is this one of the honey and black soap products?" he asked.

Giselle nodded and smiled. She'd been working tirelessly over the last two months. She barely slept, and Ian had to make sure she ate. Even then, her appetite was nearly non-existent. The only time she'd stopped working was when she caught the flu; and that was only because he had to make her see reason, convincing her she couldn't go into work and spread her sickness.

She was determined to get the new line out with the rest of the new products, even though he insisted it could roll out in the second or third wave of new product releases.

"Smell it," she said, eagerly. He lifted her arm higher and sniffed.

"What do you think?" she asked.

"I think...this makes me...want to take you in the supply closet and taste you," he whispered in between kisses he peppered up her arm.

She pulled her arm away and shook her head. "Behave yourself, Mr. Noble," she said. She lowered her voice and added, "You almost got us caught the other day in the office."

"I was under the desk," he reminded her, with a grin that caused tingles to form between her legs at the memory. "And everyone was gone to lunch."

"But if they were here, they would have heard for sure," she whispered back.

Ian shrugged. "It's not my fault that you're extremely vocal."

Ever since their conversation on the rooftop, followed by the out of this world sex, things had only gotten better between Ian and Giselle. They managed to grow even closer. Ian realized that he was developing feelings for his wife that he'd never had for another woman. His connection with her had been different from the beginning, but now...he felt something for her deep inside. She was burrowing herself into his heart.

"Are you ready for the bakery grand opening this weekend?" Ian asked.

"Yes," Giselle said. "When I swung by Everetts' on the way home yesterday, Tessa seemed so nervous."

"She'll be fine. Everything's going to perfect," Ian said with a smile.

"And are you ready to film the first episode of your show?" she asked.

The production crew had come up to Sweet Rapids several times to plan out how they would set up for the show. Filming would begin early the next week.

"Yes," he said with a nod.

"You're going to do an amazing job."

The faith Giselle had in him stirred something in Ian's soul.

"Thank you," he said, and watched Giselle cover her mouth to stifle a yawn. "You look exhausted, Gi."

"I'm fine, Ian."

"Baby, you don't look fine," Ian said lowering his voice, as rubbing her arm.

"It's just the last bit of the flu running its course."

"Maybe you should go to the doctor," he suggested.

Giselle sighed. "Ian, I'm going to the doctor next month."

Her yearly appointment with her oncologist was coming up and she seemed to be stressing about that. He'd done some research after Giselle revealed to him that she'd previously had cancer and learned that the chances of recurring cancer lessened more and more after the first ten years. But the chances of getting a second cancer were startling. So he empathized about her nervousness.

"I know, sweetheart," he said, rubbing her shoulders "But this–"

"Is nothing."

"If you haven't shaken this by next week, you're going to the doctor."

Giselle opened her mouth to argue, but he stopped her. "Don't argue. I'll call your mother," he threatened.

Her eyes grew wide. "You wouldn't."

"You know I would."

"Fine," she acquiesced.

The grand opening to Everetts' Bakery in Carson City went off without a hitch. Tessa and Dana outdid themselves and it was obvious that their parents, Emmett and Janet, were tremendously proud by the way their faces beamed all day. Even Aiden had shown up, with flowers for all of the women. When he'd given Dana her bouquet, he smiled, congratulated her and then pressed a kissed to her cheek before turning to leave.

Ian could tell Giselle hated seeing her friend look so sad on what was supposed to be such a happy day.

They'd swung by to grab some of the bakery's amazing treats and wish the family well on their success and then later that evening, everyone congregated at Isaiah and Tessa's home on Lake Tahoe to celebrate more.

"Giselle doing okay?" Isaiah asked, walking up to Ian who was standing off in a corner watching Giselle chat with Tessa, Dana, Janet and Irene.

"If you have to ask..." Ian said, shaking his head before taking a sip of his champagne. "She's running herself ragged man. She's losing weight from barely eating. And every time I suggest she rest, or even just slow the hell down, she wants to try and argue."

"Has she gone to the doctor?"

"I think doctors make her antsy. You know because of the

whole cancer thing..." He'd confided in his brother when he learned about Giselle having childhood leukemia. "It seems like she only goes when she deems it absolutely necessary. But I put my foot down and told her if she's not feeling better by next week, she's going. Even if I have to throw her over my shoulder and take her."

"Good. Look at you," Isaiah said, with a teasing grin.

"Look at me...what?" Ian asked, confused.

"You're like this loving, doting husband. If I didn't know better, I'd swear it was the real deal between the two of you."

Ian sighed. "Yeah well, maybe it's becoming realer than either of us planned."

"Did my ears deceive me?" Isaiah said in a hushed tone. "Are you telling me you might *actually* love your wife?"

Giselle chose that exact moment to look his way. She gave him a sweet smile before she returned her focus to the conversation between the other four women.

"I think I just might," he admitted for the first time out loud.

The light clinking of a knife against a glass had everyone turning.

"That's my cue," Isaiah said, stepping away from Ian.

"Excuse me, everyone," Emmett Everett said loudly, getting everyone's attention. He held his hand out to his wife and she quickly went to his side. "On behalf of Janet and myself, I'd like to thank all of you who made this grand opening a spectacular success. Especially the two women, whom none of this would have been possible without, our daughters Tessa and Dana."

A round of applause filled the living room and when it died down, Emmett continued. "It's been a long, interesting road," he said, looking down at his wife. "It took some of us a bit of convincing to see that opening another location would be a good idea."

"A *lot* of convincing," Dana said out loud, causing chuckles around the room.

"Yes," Janet admitted. "I was not on board with some of the girls' ideas in the beginning. But I've since learned the err of my ways. And I'd be remiss if I didn't say how extremely proud I am of both of you. Your father and I love you."

"To Everetts' Bakery," Emmett boasted.

"To Everetts' Bakery," everyone echoed.

Isaiah took Tessa's hand and pulled her to the middle of the living room and her parents stepped out of the way for them.

"I'd just like to add how proud I am as well," he said, turning to Tessa. "You've worked so hard to make this happen. I've seen the blood, sweat and tears you've poured into this. On top of all of that, you were there for me during one of the toughest times in my life. I have no doubt that this new endeavor you're embarking on will be a complete success. And I would be a fool if I didn't want to take the journey with you as my wife."

The room gasped collectively, as Isaiah bent down on one knee and opened a velvet ring box.

"Tessa Everett, will you–"

"Yes! Yes! Yes!" she said, hopping up and down.

The room filled with applause and Isaiah slid the ring on to Tessa's trembling finger and then stood, taking her in his arms for a searing kiss.

Ian went and hugged the newly engaged couple.

"Congrats," he said. He patted his brother on the back. "Took you long enough."

Giselle came over and hugged the two of them as well.

"I'm so happy for the two of you."

Isaiah and Tessa were passed around the room for hugs and Ian and Giselle stood back and watched, smiling.

"That was beautiful," Giselle said.

"Yeah it was."

They stayed around and partied well into the night, until Ian noticed Giselle looking tired. Then he took her home.

It had been a big day for Tessa and Isaiah.

Ian's big day was on the way.

Chapter Twenty-Eight

"Hey, I'm Ian Noble and welcome to my home."

"Cut...that was perfect, Ian."

Ian smiled and nodded.

It was Monday afternoon and Ian looked around his kitchen. They were getting ready to start shooting him as he prepared the first meal for the first episode of his cooking show. To say he was excited was an understatement. That morning, they'd done a few promo shots for commercials. The network wanted to get them airing as soon as possible.

They'd also shot video of him picking fresh vegetables for the meal as he talked about the importance of the garden to table movement.

"We'll take five and then start back with the meal prep," the director said.

Ian removed the apron and tossed it on the island and headed straight for Giselle.

"Can you believe all this?" he asked, looking around.

Giselle gave him a proud smile. "You're doing it," she said.

"Thanks to you," he whispered in her ear, before pressing a kiss to her temple. "How are you feeling?"

She nodded her head trying to convince him that she was fine. But he saw the weary look in her eyes. She was trying not to worry him.

"Gi–"

"Ian, this is *your* day."

He opened his mouth to speak, but the director called out to him.

"Ian, we need you back at the island."

"Go," Giselle said, smiling.

He gave her another kiss and then went back to the island so they could start back filming.

Giselle stood off to the side, watching Ian in the kitchen as he chopped vegetables and gave instructions for the dish he was making. She smiled when he looked up and gave the camera a sexy grin.

"This is what he was meant to do," Michelle said, standing next to Giselle.

"It seems that way," she replied.

The film crew had arrived early that morning to set up. There were so many people and so many cameras. But Ian took it all in stride; he was used to it after previously being on a cooking show.

But this time, it was all about him.

The stage manager came over to Giselle.

"Do you remember your cue?" she asked. "It's almost time."

Giselle nodded. The stage manager smiled and gave her arm a warm squeeze. "Remember, just go with the flow. Try to be as natural as possible."

Giselle nodded again and moved closer to the mark she'd been assigned to. She was supposed to walk over to the island

and ask Ian what he was making. They'd have a little flirty banter, along with him giving her a taste test, and then she'd walk off again. She would make another appearance when the meal was 'ready' and they would sit down at the dining room table to eat together.

Giselle placed her hand on her forehead and blew out a breath. Her body felt jittery and she tried to shake the feeling. There was no reason for her to have stage fright; she'd performed live countless times.

She heard her cue and went to take a step forward when the room began to spin. The last thing she remembered was Ian dropping what was in his hands and rushing to her as her world went black.

Giselle moaned and a familiar beeping sound filled her ears. Her eyes slowly opened and Ian's worried face was the first thing she saw.

"Ian?"

"Hey, baby," he said, moving closer to her. "How are you feeling?"

"What happened?"

"You passed out at the house. We brought you to the hospital."

"Oh no! Your show."

Ian shook his head. "We halted production. We'll start back when you're feeling better."

Before Giselle could say anything else, there was a light knock on the door.

Giselle's eyes grew wide when her oncologist entered the room.

"Dr. Bailey?"

"Hey, Giselle," she said, smiling as she moved to stand over Giselle's hospital bed. "I received a page that you were admitted. I spoke to your husband and he told me about how you've been feeling under the weather the last few weeks."

"I've been putting a lot of extra hours in at work, and I caught some cold or flu. It took a while to shake, but it's passing."

"Well let's give you a look and see what we can do to get you out of here as soon as possible."

Dr. Bailey began to exam Giselle and after a few minutes, she took a step back and wrapped her hands around her stethoscope.

"It feels like your spleen may be slightly enlarged. And your lymph nodes seem to be swollen quite a bit."

Giselle sat up in bed.

"But those things are normal right? Lymph nodes swell all of the time."

"Yes, it's normal, usually. And your spleen could just be doing its job and is overactive. But with your medical history, these things *can* be red flags."

Panic set in at her doctor's words.

"Look, I don't want you to worry. It could be nothing. It probably *is* nothing. But, I want to go ahead and get some blood work done on you. Just to rule the worst case scenario out. You were scheduled for your yearly appointment in a few weeks anyway, right?"

Giselle nodded her head numbly.

"Okay," Dr. Bailey said. "Then we'll just do it early. Hang tight, I'll send a nurse in."

"Can I go home?" she asked. She was tired, frustrated and now scared.

Dr. Bailey smiled. "I don't see why not. Everything else looks good," she looked at Ian. "See that she doesn't do too much."

Ian nodded quietly.

"I'll give you a call when we have the blood work back. It shouldn't take any more than twenty-four hours; forty-eight if the lab is backed up."

After Dr. Bailey left, Giselle sighed.

"I still can't believe I ruined your show."

"You didn't ruin anything. The show can wait."

"What do you mean 'the show can wait'?"

"Giselle," Ian said. "Your health is what is most important to me right now."

"But your show should be what's most important right now."

Ian's head reared back as if she'd just slapped him.

"How could you even think anything is more important than you? You're...you're my wife."

"Exactly. I'm your wife, because I agreed to stay married to you so you could get your show."

"I'm not about to argue with you about this right now," he said turning away from her.

"Ian, this show is all you've ever wanted."

"Maybe that's not all that I want anymore, Giselle," he said, looking at her over his shoulder.

The nurse chose that moment to walk in.

"Hey there," he said. "I'm here to take your blood. After that, we'll get your discharge papers and you'll be good to go."

Half an hour later, Giselle had given several blood samples and was brought a wheelchair to help her out of the hospital.

"I don't need that," she insisted.

"Don't be stubborn, Gi," Ian said.

She was helped into the wheelchair and they rolled her out to Ian's car.

When they arrived at home, Giselle was surprised to see there wasn't a trace of the camera crew left in the house. She would have never known they'd been there earlier in the day had she not seen it with her own eyes.

Ian helped her upstairs.

"I'm going to take a shower," she said, quietly.

"Do you need anything?" Ian asked.

She shook her head and made her way to the bathroom.

She'd tried her best not to let the idea that her cancer had returned, or that a new one was invading her body, fester.

But she was failing miserably. And it terrified her.

It had been nearly an hour since Giselle had gone into the bathroom and Ian was starting to worry. Unable to wait a second longer, he crossed the bedroom in several strides and pushed the en suite door open.

He froze when he saw Giselle on the floor in the shower, the water cascading over her body as she hugged her legs tightly.

"Gi," he said, rushing to her and kneeling. "Are you okay? Are you hurt?"

She lift her head slowly, her hair plastered to her face and Ian saw her bloodshot eyes.

"I can't go through it again," she said, her bottom lip trembling as she frantically shook her head. "I can't go through it again."

Ian reached up, turned off the water and then grabbed a towel off of the warming rack.

He wrapped her body in the towel and then picked her up and took her to the bed.

He laid her in the bed, holding her tightly as her entire body wracked with sobs.

"Hey," he said, when her crying calmed to quiet hiccups. "Whatever happens, I got you. Okay?"

She didn't speak, but she nodded.

"You once told me that we're in this together. And while at the time, you were talking about this agreement that, if you really think about it, is kinda fucked up..." He was glad to see that drew out a tiny smile from her. "You have to know that I wouldn't change a thing. And you mean a whole hell of a lot more to me than some show."

He kissed her forehead and pulled her close again, praying to God that the blood work would come back good.

Not for his sake, but for Giselle's.

Chapter Twenty-Nine

She was rolling her tongue ring against her teeth rapidly. Ian reached over and took Giselle's hand in his.

"Gi–"

"This is bad..." she said quietly. "This is *so* bad."

"Calm down, baby," he said in a soothing tone. "Even Dr. Bailey said it was probably nothing."

"That was *two* days ago. Before they ran the tests," she said. The lab ended up being backed up, so it took longer to get the results back. "Ian, they don't call you in for your results if it's good. Most of the time, they just call you up and say, 'Hey your blood work's good. See you next year'. This is bad."

They were sitting in Dr. Bailey's office after getting a call to come in.

Giselle had been a wreck. First, because of the extended waiting and then because of the call they received earlier that morning. But Ian had been her rock through everything. He'd offered to call her family, but she didn't want to alarm them over what could be nothing.

But sitting in this office meant it was *something*. She went to stand and pace the room, but Ian gripped her hand tighter.

"Giselle, you need to breathe, sweetheart."

Giselle was in full panic mode.

"Ian...you didn't sign up for this. Having a wife with cancer, if you want to bow out–"

"Hey!" he said firmly, as he grabbed her chin and forced her to look at him. "We talked about this last night. We're in this together. No matter what happens. If you're still in, so am I. I'm not going anywhere, Giselle, okay?"

"Okay," she said, nodding her head. Her lip began to tremble, as she whispered, "Ian, I'm scared."

Ian pulled her into his arms and rocked her. "I know, baby. I'm scared for you."

The office door swung open and Dr. Bailey came in and sat down at her desk.

"Good morning, Giselle. I'm sure you're ready for the results."

Giselle nodded, as she gripped Ian's hand.

"Your blood work came back pretty normal; your white blood cell count wasn't low. In fact, it was elevated."

"Sooo...the cancer didn't come back?" Giselle asked.

"No," Dr. Bailey said. "You're still in remission from the leukemia and there are no signs of any other cancers."

Relief washed over Giselle and she let out the breath she'd been holding.

She looked over at Ian as he asked Dr. Bailey, "You said her white blood cell count was elevated. Is that good or bad?"

"It means her body is fighting off the infection she's had for the last few weeks. Which, according to the results..." she said, looking down at the chart. "Appears to be mononucleosis."

Both Giselle and Ian's eyes grew wide.

"Mo–mono? *That's* what's been making me sick all this time?" she asked.

"I thought that was just something horny little teenagers got from kissing all of the time," Ian said, dumbfounded.

Dr. Bailey smiled. "That's a common misconception. While yes, it's most often seen in children and teenagers, everyone is susceptible to it. And you can get it from more than just kissing. If you've been around someone who's coughed or sneezed without properly covering their mouth, or drank from a public water fountain, you could have easily contracted it."

Giselle shook her head. "I'm never drinking from a water fountain again."

Dr. Bailey went. "The truth of the matter, is we can never really tell *how* you got it. For all we know, Ian, you could have had it first, but your symptoms were so mild you just never knew. You should consult with your doctor as well, just to make sure you're fine. With the way you described Giselle's work habits lately, the added stress may have just made her case more severe."

"So what do we do?" Ian asked.

Dr. Bailey looked at Giselle. "You *rest*," she said firmly.

"I can do that," Giselle said, nodding. "Easing up on overtime at work and–"

"No, Giselle. I mean bed rest."

Giselle's eye grew even wider. "You're...you're kidding right? You're putting me on bed rest...for *mono*?"

"For three weeks."

"Are you out of your fucking mind?!"

"Giselle!" Ian scolded.

Dr. Bailey was unbothered by Giselle's outburst. "Remember yesterday, I also said your spleen felt enlarged? You need to limit your physical activity and keep your stress levels down to...non-existent. Yes, it seems like mononucleosis is not a big deal, and generally it isn't. But the fact is, if you don't rest like you should, it *could* become a big deal. You could rupture your spleen and then have to have surgery. If we have to remove it, it will make it harder for you to fight off infections. You're actually quite lucky you didn't have to have it removed during your bout with leukemia. So yes, three weeks bed rest. And it will probably be another month or two before you're feeling at your best."

"She'll rest," Ian insisted, looking at Giselle.

Giselle was frustrated that she wouldn't be able to do anything for nearly a month. Then she gasped and looked at Ian. "The reception!" It was coming up soon.

"We'll postpone it," Ian assured, her. "Mom will take care of everything. We'll have it when you're feeling better."

Giselle sighed. She was actually looking forward to it more than she probably should, all things considered.

"Thank you, Dr. Bailey," she said. While she was disappointed that she would be missing out on a lot of things, she had to remember the bright side of things. She was still cancer free.

They went to stand when Dr. Bailey held up her hand.

"I'm actually not quite done with the news."

They slowly sat down and waited for Dr. Bailey to continue.

"Another reason you should make sure to rest and the main reason I called you in today, was to let you know that when we got the blood work back, we discovered one more thing."

"What?" Giselle said, her heart pounding in her chest.

"It seems...you're pregnant, Giselle."

"I'm sorry," Giselle said, blinking at Dr. Bailey. "I must have heard you wrong. Because I couldn't have heard you say that I was pregnant."

"You heard me right," Dr. Bailey said, smiling.

"But...the chemo from the leukemia..." she stuttered. "They told me I may not be able to have children."

This wasn't news to Ian. After she'd told him about the cancer, she'd shared more stories of what she went through during that time, including doctors telling her that there was a chance she'd never have children.

"Did they ever test you to see if you were infertile, Giselle?" Dr. Bailey asked, as she folded her hands and placed them on her desk.

Giselle shook her head. "Since I was so young, getting better was the main focus. And when I went into remission, they said if and when I decided to see if having children was possible, I could get tested then."

"Apparently it's possible," she said, smiling. "Congratulations you two. You'll need to make an appointment with your OB/GYN soon, of course."

Both Giselle and Ian sat in shock.

Dr. Bailey stood. "I have another appointment to get to. But you two stay in the office and take all of the time you need to let this process."

After the door closed, Giselle turned to look at Ian.

A baby *certainly* wasn't in the plans. How would this change their agreement? Would he be happy? Mad?

"Ian?"

He blinked and turned to look at Giselle. He was quiet as he looked at her first in her eyes, and then his gaze drifted down to her belly.

"A baby," he murmured.

"We haven't used protection since we got married," she blurted out.

"No," he said, grinning. "We haven't."

"This is big. I know it's a lot to take in–"

He grabbed her face and pulled her to him, kissing her.

She shoved him away, covering her mouth. "Ian! The mono!"

"Damn that," Ian said. "I'm kissing my wife."

He smiled brightly as he caressed her cheek. "Gi...you're fucking pregnant!"

A wide grin spread across her face.

"I'm fucking pregnant!"

Epilogue

Giselle was finishing up her make up when Ian walked into the bedroom. She looked spectacular in her long evening gown, her ever growing breasts spilling over the top. He ran his hands down the jacket of his tuxedo.

He locked eyes with Giselle in the mirror and she smiled at him.

"Don't you look sexy," she said, turning to face him.

"And you look gorgeous, as usual."

"No thanks to you," she said, playfully glaring at him. "I've got like a pound of cover up on my neck to hide all the hickey's you put there. I looked like a fucking cheetah."

It had been two months since their surprise at the doctor's office. While Ian had been stunned, he was amazed when he realized that he was also excited about finding out Giselle was pregnant.

When they got home, Ian made sure Giselle rested and he waited on her hand and foot. Giselle fussed constantly, but he mostly told her to shut up and let him take care of his wife and baby.

The rest had paid off because now Giselle was healthier

than ever. She'd gained back the weight she'd lost and then some, thanks to the pregnancy and Ian loved every curvy, sexy inch. She was filling out even more, and Ian couldn't keep his hands or mouth off of her.

And now they were getting ready to head to the reception they'd previously postponed.

Giselle's family flew in from North Carolina and Ian had a great time getting to know them. He loved seeing the connection between Giselle and her sister.

"The limo is on its way," Ian said. The reception was being held at Noble Estates.

"I'm ready," Giselle said, picking up her purse.

She moved to head for the door when Ian grabbed her wrist.

"Before we head out, I need to talk to you."

Giselle turned and looked at him.

"Is everything okay, Ian?"

"Yes...no." Ian shook his head. "Shit."

"What's wrong?" Giselle asked, sounding nervous.

"Do you know what today is?" Ian asked.

Giselle smiled. "Of course," she said. "It's been six months since we lost our damn minds, got drunk and married."

"Gi, I fucked up."

Giselle froze. "What do you mean you fucked up? Ian...what did you do?"

He took her left hand and held it up. "All this time, I've been letting you run around with this piece of shit ring we must have bought at the drive through chapel. After everything we've been through, I should have gotten you something better a long time ago."

"Oh...is that what's bothering you?"

Giselle slid her arms up and around his neck. "Ian...I love *you*. I don't care about some stupid ring."

"And I love you. But you deserve the best."

He reached into his pocket and pulled out a large solitaire diamond.

"But if you don't care about some stupid ring, then–"

"Holy shit!" she exclaimed.

Ian chuckled as he pulled the old ring off of her finger and slid the new one on. "I guess that means you like it."

"Ian," she said, her eyes tearing up. She'd been doing that a lot since her pregnancy. "It's beautiful."

She pushed up on her toes and kissed his lips.

His phone beeped and he pulled it out of his pocket.

"That's the limo."

Half an hour later, they walked in the large tent set up in the enormous backyard to applause and cheering.

Ian was surprised to see both of his sisters rushing to him. He pulled them into a large group hug, squeezing them tightly.

"What are you two doing here?"

"We weren't going to miss this!" Isabella said.

"You two look like the real deal," Ivy whispered, with a grin. There were no secrets between him and his siblings, so they'd known the truth as well.

Ian looked over at Giselle and then back to his sister.

"It may not have been in the beginning," Ian said. "But it definitely is now."

Giselle came over and was greeted with hugs and congrats by both of Ian's sisters.

Irene gave a short greeting, and then dinner was served. During the meal, Giselle's family took their turns giving speeches and then Isaiah did as well.

Once the meal was done, Ian and Giselle cut the cake and fed it to each other. Giselle laughed when Ian smeared a little icing on her lips before kissing it off.

"Speech!" someone yelled to Ian. He took the mic that someone handed him and stood, pulling Giselle up with him.

"First of all, I'd like to thank everyone for coming out to

celebrate with us. We have a lot more to celebrate now. Of course, our family is aware, but we wanted to wait until tonight to share with the rest of you all who are near and dear to us that we will be adding a new member to the Noble family," he said, wrapping his arm around Giselle and planting his hand over her stomach.

The tent was filled with gasps and then applause.

"At Home with Ian will be adding another little cast member in about six months. Which, by the way, season one premieres in a few weeks so check your local listings for show-times," he said with a wink that garnered laughter from the crowd.

"It's been a whirlwind," Ian said, smiling. "I never would have imagined my life would turn out this way, but I'm grateful for it every day. Giselle, you are the best thing that has ever happened to me. I was lost until I found you. And I will spend the rest of my life taking care of you and making sure you always feel cherished. I love you so much, sweetheart."

Giselle's eyes glittered with tears.

"I love you too."

He bent down and kissed her deeply and then they made their way to the dance floor.

They danced the night away with family and friends, who'd joined them to celebrate something that had started off as what could have quite possibly been the biggest mistake in his life but turned out to be the best thing he'd ever done.

The End

Thanks for reading!

Book by Té

McAllister Friends

Dream Lover
Taking Chances
Always You

McAllister Family Series

After the Storm
Just One Kiss
Perfection
Love After War
Just One Night
Just Once Touch
Book 7 (2016)

The Coalton, Texas Novella Series

Homecoming
Sanctuary

Reawakening
Destined
Irresistible

Four Seasons of Love Series

A Spring Affair
Sultry Summer Nights
Autumn Kisses
A Winter Rendezvous

In The Line of Love Series

Let Me Love You
Love's Taken Over

The Nobles of Sweet Rapids

Noble Love
Noble Surrender
Noble Seduction (TBD)
Noble Conclusions (TBD)
Keep in touch!

Facebook: www.facebook.com/TeRussNovels & www.facebook.com/TeRussAuthor
Twitter: www.twitter.com/TeRussNovels
Blog: www.terussnovels.blogspot.com
Email: terussnovels@gmail.com

Noble Surrender

Published by Shanté Russ

Made in the USA
Columbia, SC
06 June 2025

59007238R00126